Oh, yes, she liked this man a lot....

"Thanks," Blythe told Lee.

"For what?"

"For everything. But mostly, for not judging or thinking too harshly of me." She laughed. "Or at least for not showing it, if you do think I'm a horrible person."

There was a short silence before Lee glanced at her again, the frown still putting lines between his eyes. "I don't think you're a horrible person." He said the words as if he meant them.

Blythe smiled, more pleased than she could tell him. "It wouldn't surprise me if you did. But I didn't think you considered me the world's biggest creep, since you always make me feel that you're giving me the benefit of the doubt. Or at least trying to."

"I am."

"It means a lot to me. And as I said before, what I've done isn't as bad as it seems," she said quietly.

Dear Reader,

Welcome to Silhouette **Special Edition** . . . welcome to romance. Each month, Silhouette **Special Edition** publishes six novels with you in mind—stories of love and life, tales that you can identify with—romance with that little "something special" added in.

And may this December bring you all the warmth and joy of the holiday season. The holidays in Chicago form the perfect backdrop for Patricia McLinn's *Prelude to a Wedding,* the first book in her new duo, WEDDING DUET. Don't miss the festivities!

Rounding out December are more stories by some of your favorite authors: Victoria Pade, Gina Ferris, Mary Kirk and Sherryl Woods—who has written Joshua's story— *Joshua and the Cowgirl,* a spinoff from *My Dearest Cal* (SE #669).

As an extraspecial surprise, don't miss *Luring a Lady* by Nora Roberts. This warm, tender tale introduces us to Mikhail—a character you met in *Taming Natasha* (SE #583). Yes, Natasha's brother is here to win your heart—as well as the heart of the lovely Sydney Hayward!

In each Silhouette **Special Edition** novel, we're dedicated to bringing you the romances that you dream about—the types of stories that delight as well as bring a tear to the eye. And that's what Silhouette **Special Edition** is all about—special books by special authors for special readers!

I hope you enjoy this book and all of the stories to come.

Sincerely,

Tara Gavin
Senior Editor

VICTORIA PADE
Over
Easy

 Silhouette Special Edition

Published by Silhouette Books New York

America's Publisher of Contemporary Romance

SILHOUETTE BOOKS
300 East 42nd St., New York, N.Y. 10017

OVER EASY

ISBN: 0-373-09710-7

First Silhouette Books printing December 1991

Printed in the U.S.A.

Books by Victoria Pade

Silhouette Special Edition

Breaking Every Rule #402
Divine Decadence #473
Shades and Shadows #502
Shelter from the Storm #527
Twice Shy #558
Something Special #600
Out on a Limb #629
The Right Time #689
Over Easy #710

VICTORIA PADE,

bestselling author of both historical and contemporary romance fiction, is the mother of two energetic daughters, Cori and Erin. Although she enjoys her chosen career as a novelist, she occasionally laments that she has never traveled farther from her Colorado home than Disneyland, instead spending all her spare time plugging away at her computer. She takes breaks from writing by indulging in her favorite hobby—eating chocolate.

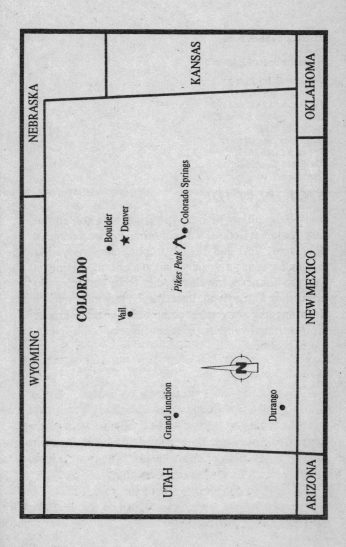

Chapter One

"Why do you keep looking at your watch?" Blythe Coopersmith asked her brother when she caught him doing it for the fourth time since they'd entered the lumberyard of the building supply store.

Rather than answering her question, Gib asked one of his own. "Why can't you just pick out a door without scrutinizing each one?"

"This will be the entrance to my home," she explained. "The first thing everyone sees when they come to visit. It has to be just right." Blythe watched her brother roll his eyes. She decided to ignore it and regarded the selection of doors again. "The trouble is that I like the one with the beveled glass in it."

"We already know that's out of the question."

"How about the white door with just the little fanlight window way up on top?"

The expression on her brother's handsome face was grim. "Don't risk it, Blythe. Get a solid one."

"This situation won't go on forever, you know. And I'll be stuck with whatever door I choose, long after my life has returned to normal," she said. But she moved on to two walnut-stained panels anyway, one plain and the other with a sprig of wheat painted on it.

The mid-May sun was beating down on their backs and the thick fall of her curly auburn hair was beginning to stick to her neck. Blythe caught her unruly mane in both hands and held it up while she judged the merits and demerits of the next two doors. "The plain one is too plain and I don't know about the wheat on the other. I like it, but would I get tired of it?" she said more to herself than to her brother.

It was all the encouragement Gib apparently needed to step up to the panel and knock on it. "It's hollow," he said with finality. "Not safe enough."

As Blythe went back to the set on her right she saw Gib glance at his watch again. "You don't have to get back for anything, do you? I'd hate to have you rush through this." She also hated the faint tremor of tension she could hear in her voice.

"Don't worry. We're going to make your house as secure as Fort Knox. I just didn't think it was going to take so long to *shop*."

Blythe laughed at the misery he put into that last word. "Poor baby," she said, linking her arm through his. Then, seriously, she went on. "I'm sorry you had to miss work this afternoon. I know finals and graduation are coming up, you're in the middle of registration and fundraising for next year, and you're swamped. It's a rotten time for the headmaster of Hale Boys' Boarding School to take off."

Gib shook his head and smiled reassuringly at her. "Missing a few hours is no big deal." He gave her a playful nudge with his shoulder. "I just wish you'd get this show on the road so we can go home and hang the door—*any* door."

She moved past three black-lacquered panels. "I know this is a pain in the neck and it would be easier if I just stayed with you and Gail."

"No, you were right about that. It isn't a good idea to bring this onto the campus. I just wish my contract didn't force me to live in the house there, so Gail and I could move in with you."

"Where would I put you? I only have one bedroom."

"I guess you'd just have to let us use it, and you'd have to sleep in the bathtub like you did that weekend you came to stay with me in college."

Blythe made a pained face. "Thanks, but no thanks. That nearly killed me then and I was seventeen. Imagine what it would do to my poor thirty-five-year-old bones now. Anything would be better than that."

"Easy to say when it's broad daylight and you're out in the open with me and a dozen other people around. You weren't so brave last night."

Blythe stepped back from a walnut door and chose not to respond to her brother's comment. Then out of the corner of her eye she saw Gib look at his watch yet again. "Are you sure you're not in a hurry?"

"I just figured we'd be home—" he looked at his wristwatch once more "—at least fifteen minutes ago."

Blythe shrugged and squinted at him. "I didn't know there was a schedule."

"Well, there is."

"Why?"

Gib's stubborn silence piqued her curiosity and as he knocked on a few other panels she watched him.

Her older brother was only about five inches taller than her own five foot four. He was stocky, squarely built, and had the same thick, reddish-brown hair she did. His eyes were not quite as black as hers, and while her face was thin and high boned, his was rounder.

He had something up his sleeve. She was sure of it.

"Why is there a schedule if you don't have to get back to the school today? And what difference does it matter that we're fifteen minutes off it?"

He didn't look at her and didn't answer for so long she wasn't sure he'd heard her. Then he threw a glance in her general direction without actually meeting her eyes and said, "I didn't want to tell you this until we were headed for home."

"What?" she demanded suspiciously.

"We have an appointment that we're going to be late for unless we can make it home in the next ten minutes."

"An appointment for what?"

"I hired you a bodyguard."

Blythe laughed. "Sure you did." She moved on to the next bin of doors.

"I did, Blythe," Gib confirmed as he followed her.

"You have to be kidding."

"I'm not."

He sounded serious and for the first time she took him that way. "Why would you hire me a bodyguard?"

"Why are we here?" he asked, then answered his question before she could. "We're here to replace your front door with one that doesn't have a window in it, so that when Howard comes back for a second try he can't just break the glass, reach through it to unlock the door and let himself in, the way he did last night."

Blythe cringed at the blunt summary of the past evening's events. "We don't know for sure that it was Howard."

"Don't we?"

Okay, so they did. "Well, anyway, I don't need a *bodyguard*." She exaggerated the word to make it sound as ridiculous as she thought it was.

"I think you do."

Blythe shook her head. "Howard isn't dangerous. The new door is all the precaution I need."

"No, it isn't. A new door can't protect you when you're coming or going from the house. It can't protect you if he breaks a window and comes in that way."

Blythe jammed her hands into her jeans pockets and headed for an oak panel she liked. "It'll be okay," she said a little feebly. "Besides, don't forget that I don't have an income at the moment. I certainly can't pay for a bodyguard, of all things."

Gib followed her. "It's my treat. Gail and I discussed it and agreed that it was worth it to us to know you're being taken care of. Call it an early birthday present if you want."

"I don't need to be taken care of. Howard wouldn't hurt me."

"You don't know that. You were just lucky you weren't home last night. What if you're not that lucky again? And if Howard would break the window, come into your house and ransack the place, there's no telling what else he might do. You can't deny that."

Maybe she couldn't. "Still, I don't need some big ape shadowing my every move."

"If Howard resorted to physical force, could you stop him?"

Or blame him? she asked herself. "This is a delicate situation, Gib. It can't be handled with brute strength."

"But if brute strength is necessary, I want to know it's available to you. I called an agency this morning and they're sending a man over to your house for us to meet. So pick a door and let's get home before we miss the guy," he said as if that ended the discussion.

Blythe pointed to an oak panel with concentric squares carved into it. "I'll take this door but I don't want a bodyguard," she informed him.

Gib wrote the number of the door on the slip of paper he'd been given, so they could pay for it inside and then pull the truck into the yard to pick it up. "Think of him as protecting the formula if it makes you feel better."

Thoughts of the formula definitely didn't make her feel better. "This is all your fault, you know," she grumbled as they headed back to the warehouselike store. "If you had played with your own toy chemistry set that year you got it for Christmas instead of giving it to me, I could have grown up to be a teacher or a secretary instead of a biochemist."

"Is that your way of accepting the bodyguard?" Gib asked as they went up to the checkout.

"No," she said emphatically. A bodyguard, of all things! Some hulking stranger living with her like a guest in a house that was barely big enough for her alone, and dogging her like a hound with the scent. Not an appealing thought, even if she could get past the melodramatic sound of the whole idea. "No bodyguard," she mouthed over her shoulder, while the clerk rang up the door and the three locks she was buying.

When she'd paid the bill they headed for the parking lot. "This is serious business, Blythe," Gib said on the way to the truck he'd borrowed from the school. "Don't underestimate Howard. And don't kid yourself. You—and the formula—need protection."

She knew her brother realized he'd hit her Achilles' heel with the formula and that he intended to use his advantage. To be honest, his proposal was something she had to consider, she thought, as Gib backed up to the loading gate and got out to give a yard worker the receipt. She didn't have any illusions about the situation she'd put herself in. Howard was not going to complacently accept what she'd done. She hadn't expected him to. Neither had she expected him to do something like what he'd done last night.

"Okay, we're all set," Gib said when he got back into the cab and put the truck into gear.

Blythe picked up the conversation where they'd left off. "A bodyguard is just going too far. I'll keep everything locked up and be careful whenever I go anywhere. And I can check in with you or Gail every hour on the hour if it'll make you feel better. But I don't want a bodyguard."

"Do you want to face Howard alone if he gets past your locked door or lies in wait for you to leave the house? Do you want to try to physically keep the formula from him? Could you fight him off?"

The answer to all of his question was no, and Blythe knew he knew it, so she said nothing.

Gib stopped at a red light and looked her in the eye. "You may have convinced yourself differently in the light of day and forgotten how upset you were when you called me last night, but I haven't. You need help, you need protection. I can't give either of those, but a bodyguard can. Besides, could you really concentrate if you were listening for every sound or wondering if Howard was around every corner?"

Again Blythe didn't answer him. Instead she had a sudden memory flash of what it had been like to come home last night and find her front door wide open—to step into that house in the dark because the lamp that was normally turned on by the nearest switch was lying broken on the floor, to wonder if someone was going to jump out at her or grab her from behind, to trip over sofa cushions and debris scattered everywhere—and finally to get a light on and go from room to room, looking at the wreckage that cluttered every corner.

"I guess I could meet the man," she conceded. "But I'd feel like an idiot walking around with a bodyguard."

"I guarantee he won't have I Am A Bodyguard tattooed across his forehead."

"He probably also won't have a neck," Blythe muttered to herself. "Or a brain."

"You win. I give up."

At his friend's words Lee Horvat cut short his run toward the facing wall of the handball court and bent over, one hand just above each knee, his head hanging, so the sweat dripped off his blond hair to the floor rather than down his face. When he'd caught his breath he straightened up, leaned against the wall and slid down beside Chad Ingalls, who was lying spreadeagled on his back, staring up at the ceiling.

"Good game," Lee said, resting his head.

Chad groaned. "Bull. I haven't played in the whole year you've been gone and it showed."

"Yeah, but I didn't want to be the one to say it." Lee grinned and jabbed his old high school buddy and present business partner with one toe of his tennis shoe.

"S'okay," Chad wheezed. "I wouldn't have traded places with you. I've had better things to do with my spare time than play handball."

"Oh sure. Like meeting a great woman, getting engaged, and buying a fancy new house together are better than being stranded in Oregon to build a bridge, without knowing anybody or having anything to do in the few off-hours but scrounge up a handball game."

Chad's chubby face lighted up in a beatific smile. "Yeah, what could I have been thinking?"

"And don't forget you still owe me for using that two-headed coin in the toss that got me stuck going to Oregon, while you stayed here."

"So what do you want to do about it? Dissolve the partnership that's been working for us both since we got out of engineering school?" Chad goaded him.

"And rob myself of a way to get even? Not a chance. You owe me. The next job out of state is yours—even if it's in Timbuktu and you have to leave the day after your wedding."

Chad wiped the sweat off his chin and flicked it at Lee. "Dream on. The viaduct project will keep us both here and busy for the next three years."

"Speaking of which, I'm not going to make that dinner meeting tonight. If it's absolutely necessary for me to be there we'll have to postpone." Lee hoisted himself off the floor and gave his friend a hand up.

"How come?" Chad asked as they headed for the locker room.

"There's something I have to take care of."

This time Chad's grin was one-sided. "You met a woman."

"Hardly." Lee pulled off his T-shirt at about the same time Chad did and threw it at his friend's potbelly. "Not

only did you not play handball, but you obviously didn't
do anything else, either. Except maybe hit a lot of nice
restaurants."

Chad patted his paunch proudly. "Marcie's a great
cook. Besides—" he pointed his nearly nonexistent chin
Lee's way "—it isn't handball that keeps you looking like
that. It's good genes. That's why I had to use the two-
headed coin—you have all the luck. Any day you want to
trade my five-feet-ten for your six-three, my gut for your
flat belly, my receding hairline for that thick blond stuff
of yours or my fat cheeks for your mug, you just let me
know. I'll even throw in the two-sided coin," he sneered
as he rounded the corner of the lockers, heading for the
communal shower stall.

It wasn't until they were both dressed and out in the
parking lot that Chad again brought up the meeting Lee
needed to miss. "McMartin wasn't expecting you to be
there tonight, anyway. I told him you might want some
time off after being out of town most of the last year. I
can handle it."

"Thanks," Lee said. "My aunt called late this morning and—"

But before he could go on Chad's fiancée pulled up to
the curb. Lee exchanged greetings with the slightly
chubby, red-haired Marcie as Chad got into her car.

"We're going to have a drink. Want to come?"

"No, I can't put this off." This time Lee didn't offer
the explanation he'd been about to give. He liked Marcie, but barely knew her and didn't want to tell Chad
about personal family business in front of her. "I'll talk
to you later."

"Okay."

Lee said goodbye to Marcie and closed the door. When
they'd driven off he crossed the lot to his black fastback

and got in. It felt good to be behind the wheel of his own car again, and what he really wanted to do with the rest of the afternoon was take a drive into the mountains and enjoy the spring sunshine. But he couldn't do that, and what he had planned was much less pleasant.

He took a slip of paper off the passenger seat and read the address he'd written there when his aunt had called. Then he started the car and headed for the highway.

How the hell was he supposed to get Howard's formula back? he asked himself for what must have been the tenth time since Aggie's phone call. And how could anyone have stolen from Howard?

His aunt and uncle were two of the genuinely good people in the world, and Lee knew he was walking evidence of that fact. He didn't even want to think about what he would have done if they hadn't taken him in when he was fourteen, after both of his parents had been killed in that car accident. But they had done more than just take him in. They'd nurtured him through his grief, and had been patient enough to stand by him through some adolescent scrapes, in spite of the fact that they had three of their own kids to contend with. They'd loved and cared for him, accepting him into their family as if there were no question that he belonged with them from the moment they'd heard about the accident. There weren't many people who would have done that.

And it wasn't as if Howard and Aggie's goodness and generosity had exclusively benefited him, Lee thought when he reached his exit. No one in need who ever came to his aunt and uncle's attention went without help in some form or another. Blythe Coopersmith should know that firsthand.

How could she, of all people, turn on Howard?

"Bitch," he muttered to himself, feeling a swell of anger rise, as fresh as it had been after Aggie's anxious call last night.

Had it not been for Howard, Blythe Coopersmith would never have found work in her field again after that scandal five years ago. Howard had been the only person around not to believe she had tried to grab half the credit, money and glory for the discovery of a revolutionary diet drink patented by another scientist. It had been Howard who had taken her into his independent research group, Howard who had stood by her, even when it meant losing some of the backing for his own work.

"And how did Coopersmith thank him?"

This time, instead of making an unsubstantiated claim to someone else's accomplishment, she'd gone so far as to walk out of the lab a week ago with the only existing notes on six years of work and the completed formula for a breakthrough in weight research. Howard's breakthrough.

Apparently Miss Blythe Coopersmith had earned the bad reputation that should have ended her career five years ago.

But how was he going to get the formula back? Lee asked himself again.

He still had no idea. All he knew was that with his cousins living out of state, his aunt hadn't had anyone else to turn to. She'd been frantic as she explained that she and Howard hadn't wanted to tell him what was going on when he'd stopped by their house on his way home from the airport two days ago, because Howard had been so sure he could solve this problem on his own. But Howard had gone out last night for one more attempt to get Coopersmith to answer her door, to talk to him, to persuade her to give him back what was rightfully his.

"I didn't realize how upset your uncle actually is," Aggie had said. "But when no one answered the door again he broke a window and let himself in to try to find the formula for EASY. He cut his hand and he still didn't get his papers. He's just too agitated to deal with this himself, Lee. And he won't let me call the police."

Not that calling the police would do any good. Lee had been all for it—until he'd found out that for some reason Howard had neglected to take the necessary precautions to prove in court that the original idea was his. Add to that the facts that Coopersmith had very thoroughly dumped what was already mixed of the formula down the drain and taken off with all of the actual work that was on paper, and there was no way to prove any of it was his uncle's.

So there wasn't a choice. Lee had to do what he could to get the formula back himself.

He glanced at the address again, then at the street names. Turning when he found the one he was looking for, he offered himself a couple of possible ways to retrieve EASY.

Should he try reasoning with her? Maybe he should threaten her with legal action, pretend there was some kind of proof to back Howard up.

Both ideas were weak, he decided. From all accounts his uncle had already tried reasoning with her, and now she wouldn't even pick up her phone. Instead she'd let every message Howard had left on her machine go unanswered. Nor was there any sense in trying to bluff her. No doubt she knew how well she'd covered her tracks.

Lee spotted the small white clapboard ranch that sat far back from the street. A deep green carpet of lawn stretched from the curb to the bushes that lined the front and a canopy of red oak trees marked each side of the property, meeting over the steep, shake-shingled roof.

He pulled into the long driveway and stopped his car, wondering just exactly what he was about to face in the lady scientist. He'd never met the woman, but Howard had spoken of her over the years—always fondly. Lee pictured her tall and boxy, for some reason. And masculine looking. Probably homely, her hair unstyled and more than likely unkempt. And big teeth, she'd have very big teeth, he decided. Coopersmith the carnivore.

"I guess we'll see," he muttered as he got out.

Apparently the window Howard had broken was in the door, because the space was boarded up. With the exception of that, Lee admitted reluctantly as he approached, the house had a well tended, country cottage sort of appeal to it. Black shutters bracketed all the windows, flower boxes lined the bottoms, there was a fire-engine-red mailbox to the right of the coal-colored crossbuck screen, and bright yellow tulips bloomed on either side of the front stoop whose three steps he climbed. He didn't know what the home of a research pirate should look like, but this didn't strike him as it.

There was no sound coming from the house. When Lee pushed the doorbell he heard it ring. But no one came to answer it. He rang again. Then again. Nothing.

He opened the screen and tried knocking, but that didn't work any better.

Was she really not home or was she hiding in there? He leaned to the side and looked over the tiered curtains that concealed the bottom half of a picture window. Through the glass exposed by tie-back drapes above them he could see the combination living room-dining room-kitchen.

Was she such a poor housekeeper, or had Howard messed the place up that much? he wondered. If it was his uncle who'd done such damage, Howard really must have been upset.

To the left of the living room was a hallway and to the right an open door through which he could see the corner of what he assumed was either a washer or a dryer. There was no sign of Blythe Coopersmith.

Still, she could be down that hall or hiding in that laundry room.

Lee closed the screen and headed to the left. A four-poster bed dominated the room he looked into from the front and side windows, a room in as much disarray as the others had been. Two Tiffany-style lamps stood on night tables on either side of the bed, there was a hope chest at its foot and an antique armoire against one of the side walls. But there was no Blythe Coopersmith.

He went around to the back, where he found a frosted-glass window open just far enough for him to see into the small bathroom; the greenhouse window over the kitchen sink left him sure she wasn't in the laundry room, either.

"Well, she has to come home sometime," he said to himself as he headed to the front again.

No sooner had he rounded the corner of the house than a car pulled into the driveway behind his. A man of about Lee's height and build got out and rushed toward him. "You must be Mr. Coopersmith," he said in a hurry. "I'm sorry I'm so late, but I had a flat tire and no spare." He extended his hand. "I'm Roland Ames—the bodyguard the agency sent over. They said you wanted to hire me for your sister."

Lee processed that information in short order and realized that Blythe Coopersmith was about to hire a brick wall to put between herself and having to answer for what she'd done.

He shook the man's hand. "I'm sorry, but my sister has changed her mind," he said, thinking fast. "Hiring a bodyguard was my idea and I was pretty sure I had her convinced, but she had second thoughts. I'm afraid I've had you come for nothing."

"Maybe I can talk to her," the man suggested. "Some people are uncomfortable with the idea until they meet me, and if she's in real danger—"

"No," Lee cut him off. The last thing he needed was to have Coopersmith drive up while this man was still here. "That wouldn't do any good. She's made up her mind and once she has, there's no changing it. Actually she isn't in any real danger. A bodyguard was a precaution for my peace of mind more than anything and she just plain won't agree to it." Lee took out his wallet. "But I don't want to have wasted your time." He held out a fifty-dollar bill.

"That's not necessary," the man said.

Lee nearly shoved it into the bodyguard's hand. "I insist."

"You're sure you won't be needing me?"

"Positive."

The man finally took the money. "If she changes her mind—"

"I'll call. And I'll be sure to request you."

A bodyguard, Lee thought as he watched the man get into his car and back out of the driveway. "I'll give you a bodyguard," he muttered under his breath.

No. It was a crazy idea.

But then this was a crazy situation.

A bodyguard would have to keep tabs on Blythe Coopersmith's every move—and have access to the formula, most likely. It was almost too perfect.

Could it work?

Since they'd never met and Howard didn't carry pictures of his nephew, she wouldn't recognize his face. But what about his name?

When was the last time Howard had called him by anything but Bucky? To anybody? Lee had managed to get everyone else to drop the hated nickname, but had made absolutely no headway with his uncle. And surely his middle name—Farrell, his mother's maiden name— would never have come up. Blythe Coopersmith might have heard of Bucky Horvat, but he doubted that she'd ever heard of Lee Farrell.

And even if she had, he reasoned, the worst that could happen was that he would just have to go head-to-head with her, the same way he would have, anyway.

Playing bodyguard was a wild idea, but it was the only one he had.

There was no legal backing for Howard's side, Coopersmith wasn't likely to just hand over what she'd taken, and doing something heavy-handed wasn't Lee's style.

And after all, turnabout was fair play. The conniving chemist had gotten on an inside track with Howard, then betrayed him. What better way to recoup his uncle's loss than to get onto an inside track with her himself?

"Oh, good, he waited," Gib said as he pulled into Blythe's driveway behind the black car that was parked there.

Reserving judgment on whether or not that fact really was good or bad, Blythe didn't comment. Instead, she watched as the door on the driver's side of the fastback opened. "*That*'s the bodyguard?"

Dressed in well-cut khaki slacks and a red polo shirt that hugged broad shoulders, the man who got out of the car was not what she'd expected. Where was the excessively developed hulk whose head and waist should look too small in proportion to the rest of his body? Whose nose should be the smashed centerpiece of a face wearing the permanent imprints of a succession of fists? Not this guy. He was tall and athletically well built rather than muscle-bound, and even from a distance she could tell he had a fine-looking face that no violence had rearranged. Television had done bodyguards a bad turn.

Blythe climbed down from the truck at the same time her brother did and they approached the man in the driveway together.

"I'm sorry we kept you waiting," Gib said. "You are the bodyguard from the Executive Protection Agency, aren't you?"

The man smiled and extended his hand. "I'm Lee Farrell." Then he looked directly at Blythe through aquamarine-blue eyes that seemed a little cold, in spite of the polite expression on his face.

Yet even that impression didn't stop her from getting an odd little catch in her throat as she took in the sight of him at close range. He had straight blond hair that he wore just short enough and swept to one side. His eyes were deep set beneath a strong brow. His nose was a little long, but straight and perfect above lips that were neither too thin nor too full. He had a wide jaw, a square chin and high cheekbones, and when he smiled as he was doing at her, there were slight fans of lines around his eyes and two creases on either side of his mouth, both of which kept him from being too perfect. In fact, she thought, the tiny wrinkles gave his face a sort of swagger that made it all the more attractive without appearing cocky or arrogant. He was interesting looking.

But Gib was introducing her and she wasn't paying attention.

"Are you the sister who needs protecting?" Lee Farrell asked, never having taken his eyes off her.

Gib answered before she could. "She's the one."

Blythe cleared her throat. "I should tell you from the start that I'm not crazy about the idea of a bodyguard." She was also suddenly much too aware of the old jeans and plain white T-shirt she'd put on to work in today. For the life of her she couldn't imagine why what she was wearing should even occur to her.

The man smiled again. "It does seem like a pretty strange arrangement at first, but I promise I'll make you as comfortable with it as possible."

For some reason she believed he could. Gib was talking, and the bodyguard seemed slow in switching his attention to her brother.

"As I told whoever it was that I spoke to at the agency, I want someone to stay with Blythe twenty-four hours a day until further notice."

"I understand that."

Blythe finally gathered her wits enough to contribute to the interview. "How do you generally handle confrontations, Mr. Farrell?"

"Lee, please. Are we talking about offensively—as in helping you confront someone and keeping you safe while you do? Or defensively—as in putting myself between you and someone you don't want contact with?"

Articulate and intelligent. Maybe this bodyguard idea of Gib's wasn't such a bad one, after all. "I want to avoid a confrontation."

"And to keep someone from breaking into the house and getting his hands on something valuable," Gib expanded.

Lee nodded and Blythe realized that although his neck was thick and strong looking, there was a distinct definition to it; his shoulders did not bulge up to meet his hairline.

"I'm a nonviolent person, believe it or not," he answered. "I've yet to find a situation that can't be handled tactfully if some effort is put into defusing tempers."

"So you wouldn't object to a blanket rule of absolutely no strong-arming?" she asked to test him.

"Not at all. I'd object if you wanted me to do some skull bashing, but not the other way around."

"Unless the need arose. . ." Gib added.

Blythe couldn't help smiling. She nodded toward her brother but spoke to Lee in a conspiratorial aside. "He's really not as paranoid as he sounds."

The bodyguard rewarded her with a laugh that seemed to catch him unawares, chasing away the coolness in his eyes. He answered her in the same light tone. "I was wondering." Then he answered Gib. "Should things get out of control, I'd take the punches while your sister got away, but if she was adamant about my not hitting back, I wouldn't hit back," he said diplomatically.

Blythe's gaze strayed to his flat stomach and she didn't have any doubt it was hard enough to accommodate a fist without a flinch. Not that it mattered, of course.

"Well, what do you think, Blythe?"

Gib's words jolted her out of her reverie. For a moment she took him literally and tried to come up with a lie rather than admit she'd been thinking about this man's physique. Again.

"About having a bodyguard," her brother elaborated when she hesitated.

"Well..." This time she did consider his question. She wasn't happy about the idea of a bodyguard, although it was no reflection on Lee Farrell. He seemed calm and confident enough to handle himself and any situation that might arise. He was personable and intelligent, so he wouldn't be hard to have around. And certainly he was easy to look at. Maybe too easy....

Blond men didn't usually appeal to her. As a rule she went for the dark, swarthy sort. But she had to admit that there was something about this guy that proved an exception to that rule. She wasn't oblivious to his appeal—which could be a complication in a situation where they would be keeping constant company in her small house.

Still, what difference did it really make that he was an attractive man? This was only business, after all. His business protecting hers. Factoring in that she was hardly going to be knocked silly by infatuation over a handsome face or a great body, and the certainty that she could control herself, she decided that any attraction she might feel for this man wasn't really an issue.

What was an issue was the formula and keeping it away from Howard, now that she had it. This man seemed capable of doing that and doing it with kid gloves.

"Okay," she finally conceded. "If you want the job you can have it."

"Great." Gib sighed as if he had been worried she wouldn't agree.

Lee nodded. "I'll just need to arrange a few things and go home to pack." He looked at Gib. "I probably won't be able to get back here until this evening sometime. Will you be around that long?"

"I should be. I have a new front door to install. Speaking of which, before you go, I could use a little help getting it off the truck. If you wouldn't mind."

"No problem."

Blythe couldn't help watching Lee as he followed Gib. The bodyguard was as impressive looking from the back as he was from the front. His wide shoulders narrowed to a small waist, and the pockets of his pants rode a pretty terrific derriere. He also carried himself well. Very well.

"Why don't you go on up ahead and unlock the door, Blythe?" Gib suggested as they carried the new panel toward her.

She spun around and made a dash for the house, hoping neither man had realized that she'd been preoccupied—or if they had, what she'd been preoccupied with. All the same, even having already been caught in the act, she couldn't keep from turning from her opened front door to watch her new bodyguard as he carried his share of the weight. His biceps bulged, the tendons on his forearms rippled under the surface of his skin and his hands, curving around the underside of the door, were big and bony and somehow very sexy.

Then she caught herself.

So much for control.

"I won't be long," Lee said to her when he and Gib had set the door inside her house.

"No hurry," she assured him. Then she let her gaze follow him to his car as Gib backed out the truck from behind him.

Great looking, intelligent, articulate, polite, personable, diplomatic, maybe even a little charming. Why, she wondered, would a man like that choose a job as a bodyguard?

Chapter Two

"So much for how nice it was to be home again," Lee said to himself wryly as he entered his house in the outlying foothills of the Rocky Mountains west of Denver.

Tossing his car keys and the mail onto the kitchen counter, he went straight up the four steps of the split-level house to his bedroom and pulled his suitcase from the top shelf of the walk-in closet. It landed with a bounce in the center of the king-size mattress, yawning open. Then he went back to the closet and stood in front of his clothes.

How did a bodyguard dress?

It would depend, he decided, on where he was accompanying the guardee. He should have asked. A real bodyguard probably would have.

He went back down the stairs, took the phone book out of a drawer and looked up Blythe Coopersmith's number. Then he punched it in. While he listened to the ring he sorted through his mail. It was mostly junk and a few bills. He left it all sitting on top of the open phone book.

On the fourth ring a machine answered and Blythe's soft voice came on. The message was brief, to the point, and yet still friendly sounding and natural. Like the woman herself.

"Hi, this is Lee—" he almost said Horvat "—Farrell, your new bodyguard—" He stopped speaking when he heard the click of the receiver being picked up and a beep from the machine.

"I'm here," she said.

Why did she sound relieved?

"Everything okay?" he asked.

She laughed and the lilting sound reminded him of her paranoia joke about her brother's overzealous concern. Ordinarily Lee liked a woman with a sense of humor and a nice laugh. Whom was he kidding? He liked this one, too. *Keep in mind whom you're dealing with,* he told himself.

"Everything is fine," Blythe answered. "Did you call just to ask that?"

"No, I had another reason. I just didn't think you'd be this happy to hear from me."

She laughed again. "There's been a few unpleasant calls lately. I was glad this wasn't another one."

What did she expect? If he were in his uncle's shoes, Lee wasn't too sure a few unpleasant calls and ransacking her house was all he would have done in the past week.

"What's up?" she asked brightly.

"I forgot to find out how you'd like me to dress. Will we be going into an office, out on the town, or what?"

"We'll be here most of the time, so whatever you wear around your own house is fine," she said without hesitation, sounding as if she were advising a houseguest she was looking forward to entertaining. How could someone who had done what this woman had seem so warm and open and inviting?

Lee fought the urge to like her and answered a little stiffly. "That's all I needed to know. I'll be back in a while."

"There's no rush. Gib is having some trouble getting my old door off the hinges. I'm sure he'll be here a long time."

They said goodbye and hung up. For a moment Lee left his hand on the receiver, staring at it while in his mind's eye he had a clear image of Blythe.

She wasn't anything like what he'd thought she would be. Certainly she didn't look the way he'd pictured her. She wasn't tall or boxy; she was of average height and just curvaceous enough—not too thin or too plump, but just right. Just the way he liked a woman.

She was also a long way from homely with that fresh, clear, peach-colored skin and those delicate, high cheekbones. In fact there was nothing even plain about that small nose, those big, black eyes, and those pale lips that curved up slightly at the corners even when she wasn't smiling.

What was it he'd imagined her hair would be like? Unstyled and unkempt? Hardly. Instead it was neatly pulled to the back of her head, a mass of unruly russet curls, controlled as much as nature would allow.

And her teeth were small and perfect. Straight and as white as fine china. Coopersmith might be a carnivore but she didn't look it.

She wasn't what he'd expected in any other way, either. Oh, she was smart, he'd figured that, and it was true. But the last thing he had imagined was that she'd be funny, that she wouldn't take herself or anything else too seriously. That she'd be quick and witty and good-natured and...

Lee stopped himself.

She was too damn likable, that was all. He hadn't counted on that.

Too damn likable and too damn attractive.

But somewhere underneath that facade was an unethical, underhanded, conniving schemer. A person who had used Howard's trust against him.

Hanging on to that thought Lee picked up the phone and dialed another number.

"Good, I caught you. I was afraid you might have already left for dinner," he said when Chad answered.

"Five minutes from now and you'd have missed me. Speaking of which, did you tell me why you couldn't make this meeting?"

"I started to." He did now, not leaving anything out.

Chad listened, making very few comments.

"So, I'm not sure when I'll get back to work. This may take me a few days," Lee said after he'd told the whole story.

"I can't believe anybody would do something like that to your uncle."

"Neither can I." Lee was aware that his friend knew of Howard's generosity. Howard had loaned Chad interest-free tuition money to finish college when Chad's family had hit hard times and hadn't been able to help him themselves. "Anyway, besides explaining why I won't be back in the office for awhile, I called for something else. Remember that New Year's Eve party we gave five years ago? The one you brought that research assistant to?"

"Virginia. Of course I remember. She spent more time talking to Howard than she did to me. It's the only time I've had to compete with someone my father's age," Chad said wryly.

"They had something in common—they'd both worked with Blythe Coopersmith in CU's research department. Your date was pretty anxious to pass on news about the uproar involving our biochemist and some other scientist, whose name escapes me at the moment. I remember it because that was the first Howard had heard of Coopersmith's problems. He contacted her right after that and offered her a job working with him."

"Are you telling me I'm partly to blame for this mess because I brought Virginia to the party, and that's where Howard heard about this woman?"

"No, but I was wondering if you'd give the lab assistant a call—"

"Hey, I'm an engaged man. And Marcie is a jealous woman."

"I don't want you to wine and dine the lab assistant. I just want you to see how much you can find out about that old uproar."

"You think it's connected with what this woman's done to Howard?"

"I think there's definitely a pattern here. I can't remember any of the details and I'd like to know all I can about it now. It might give me some idea of the kind of person I'm dealing with."

"Somebody who's rotten to the core."

For some inexplicable reason that comment rubbed Lee the wrong way. How was that possible? he asked himself. But then how was any of what he'd been thinking in the last couple of hours possible? He'd found Coopersmith attractive, even likable. And now here he was, feeling almost defensive about her. If he'd come from somewhere farther away than Oregon in the past three days he'd think maybe jet lag was putting his reactions out of kilter. Then again, maybe it was the change in altitude; he'd spent a year at sea level, maybe there was a bigger adjustment to be made when rising a mile above it than he'd realized.

"So, you'll call the lab assistant?" Lee asked again, rather than commenting on Chad's remark about Blythe.

"You know I will. I may not tell Marcie about it, though. In fact, I'll probably call from the office, but I'll definitely call. Is there anything else I can do to help? Hold the woman down while you search her house? Menace her into telling us where the formula is? Cut up the bamboo sticks to put under her fingernails?"

"Thanks, but I think just playing her bodyguard will get me inside information about where the formula is. I'll go from there."

"She actually believed that you're a bodyguard?"

"From something called the Executive Protection Agency."

"So if I need to call you I should say I'm from there?"

"If it's an emergency. Otherwise don't call at all. I'll get back to you whenever I can to check in and find out what Virginia has to say."

"Oh, I get it. You don't trust me to play secret agent. You think I'll blow your cover," Chad teased.

"No, it's just that this whole thing is a little too weird to take any chances with. I can't say I'm comfortable pretending to be something and someone I'm not, and the less complicated it gets, the better. The last thing I need is phone calls where I have to make sure I don't say anything to give myself away."

"You're just too honest for your own good. Keep in mind that this witch swiped the biggest discovery to come out of Howard's whole career."

"That's not something I'm likely to forget." At least he was determined not to, even though he didn't understand why it should require such an effort.

"You don't think she's dangerous or something, do you?"

That made Lee laugh before he realized it was a valid question under the circumstances, coming from someone who hadn't yet met the petite chemist. "No, I don't think she's dangerous at all."

"Well, you never know. Maybe she was planted by some major drug company that knew Howard was on the brink of a great discovery."

"Pharmaceutical espionage? No, this is a lot more personal than that. This is just somebody who puts her energy into pirating other people's work, rather than accomplishing anything on her own." Why didn't it feel any better to say derogatory things about her than it did to hear them? "Anyway, just try to find out what you can for me. I'll get back to you when I have a minute alone."

"Do you want me to leave a self-destructing taped message in a phone booth for you?" his friend teased again.

"How about if I just call when I can do it without being overheard?"

"Or if you need my help," Chad said, sounding serious again.

"Or if I need your help."

This time when Lee hung up he went right back upstairs. As he folded his bathrobe he thought about sleep-

ing in that small house with Coopersmith. He'd probably
have to take the couch, while she was just a few feet down
the hall, curled up in that four-poster bed....

He pressed the back of his hand to his upper lip to blot
a little sweat that had beaded there.

Maybe he'd get lucky and she'd leave the formula lying around, so he could grab it and get out of there before bedtime.

"So what did you think of the bodyguard? Pretty nice-
looking guy, wasn't he?" Gib asked as Blythe brought
two cups of after-dinner tea and sat down beside him on
her front stoop. The new door was hung, but they'd
stopped to eat before putting in the handle and all the
locks.

"Yeah, pretty nice," she agreed vaguely, immediately
seeing through her brother.

"Actually I'd say he was very attractive."

Blythe suppressed a smile and gave him a sidelong
glance. "Have you told Gail about this appreciation you
have for men?"

"Ha, ha, ha," Gib said. But he clearly wasn't about to
be deterred. "Lee seemed like a nice person, too. And
smart."

Blythe sipped her steaming tea. "No, you're right, he
didn't fit my idea of the run-of-the-mill bodyguard," she
observed, deliberately misinterpreting what she knew
from experience was her brother's attempt at match-
making.

"No wedding ring, either."

There was obviously no way around it. She might as
well stop trying. Blythe closed her eyes and shook her
head. "Did you stipulate only single men when you called

whatever the name of that agency was for a bodyguard for me?''

"It's called the Executive Protection Agency and no, I didn't. It's just a nice bonus.''

"It's incidental.''

"Mom will be glad to hear it.'' He sounded so pleased with himself.

Blythe nodded over her shoulder toward her house. "Did you want to go in and call her, so you could share this big news?'' she teased.

"I'd like to, but I can't. Remember, you made me promise not to tell anybody what was going on.''

"So you can't very well explain why you've hired me a bodyguard, of all things,'' she went on. "Even if he is a real, honest-to-goodness, alive and breathing, available man, who just might ride in here on his white horse and save me from the perils of being—God forbid—an old maid.''

"Very funny,'' Gib said dryly. "We don't want to see you alone, that's all.''

"I like being alone.''

"No one likes being alone.''

"Who says?''

"Two by two. People were meant to go through life in pairs.''

"I never have liked pears, they're too sweet and mushy,'' she retorted, bantering like a vaudevillian, poking him in the ribs with her elbow.

"If you had a husband you wouldn't need a body-guard right now.''

"Oh, I don't know. I could have used one to protect me from good old Jerry Nickles, and he was husband material.''

Gib looked at her gravely. "Did he hit you?''

She made a face that was intended to say she thought her brother was out of his mind. "No, he didn't hit me. Do you think if he had, I wouldn't have told you until five years after the fact? I was talking metaphorically. I could have used someone to protect me emotionally and professionally."

Her brother visibly relaxed. "That's all in the past. You have to pick yourself up by the bootstraps and go on."

"I have."

"You don't even date."

"I went out in October."

"Seven months ago. And the minute you found out the guy was looking for a long-term relationship, you wouldn't see him again."

"It wouldn't have been fair. He made it clear that he was looking for someone to marry and I just wasn't bowled over by him. Simple as that. Why should I waste his time and date money when he could be out finding Ms. Right?"

"You might have liked him enough to change your mind if you would have let yourself get to know him."

"Hmm. Man as an acquired taste." She pretended to think about it, then shook her head. "Nope, sorry. I just don't think that would work."

"It wasn't love at first sight between Gail and me, either, you know."

"I'm sure Gail will be glad to hear that. The way she tells it, she knew she was going to spend the rest of her life with you five minutes after the introduction. Besides, who ever said I was looking for love? Maybe I don't want any part of it—did that ever occur to you?"

"Not *any* part of it?" he asked insinuatingly.

She laughed. "You have a dirty mind." Okay, so he was right about that. There were times when she craved to be held in a man's arms. To be kissed. Touched. Made love to.

The image of Lee Farrell came suddenly to mind.

Blythe swallowed hard and closed her eyes, as if that would block out the all too vivid visualization.

Thoughts like that would definitely not do. She was about to have the bodyguard living with her. The last thing she needed was to start having fantasies about him, for crying out loud.

But once it was there, the picture of him was difficult to get rid of. And so was the craving that had inspired it.

"Well," she said, standing up in a hurry. "Break's over. We'd better get back to work."

"You didn't answer my question," her brother reminded her.

"What question?"

"Do you really not want any part of a love relationship with a man?"

"Well, there is one thing I'd like. When my garage door breaks and I'm invariably on the outside and I have to crawl in on my stomach and then fiddle with those greasy bolts to fix it—that's the part where I'd like a man to be around, so he could do it instead of me."

"You're as funny as a crutch," Gib said as he got to his feet and handed her his empty cup. "My sister the old maid," he added, goading her under his breath, just loudly enough for her to hear it.

"That's me," Blythe said cheerfully. "Now get busy."

She took the cups back to the kitchen and rinsed them out. The thought of Lee Farrell being here in the small house with her was on her mind. What was more, that thought had caused a little tingle to skitter across her skin.

Maybe accepting his services hadn't been such a good idea, after all. But it was too late, she realized. She'd agreed, the man had been hired and was now probably on his way. She'd just have to deal with these odd reactions she had to him, she told herself as she put the cups into the dishwasher.

Gib was drilling a hole in the jamb to accommodate the thick metal of the dead bolt when Blythe went back into the living room. One look at the bolt sobered the lighter mood that had come from joking with her brother.

Who would have ever thought she'd be barring herself against Howard Horvat, let alone hiring a bodyguard to keep him away?

Howard Horvat, of all people.

She remembered the first day she'd walked into his college chemistry class and handed him her registration card. He'd teased her about her name, calling her Blythe Spirit. That had been the beginning. Howard was an incorrigible tease about everything. Nothing was sacrosanct to him. Just like her father.

God, but she was going to miss Howard!

No, that was the wrong tense. She wasn't *going* to miss him. She already missed him. She'd missed him for a long time. Ever since things had changed.

But she had to accept those changes. And the ones that were coming now. Like not working with Howard anymore, not seeing him every day, the way she had for the past five years. Changes like not having the chance to field his constant teasing or enjoy his irreverent humor. There would be no more brainstorming lunches. No more of having him to turn to when her research hit a plateau. All of that was behind her.

"What's the matter?" Gib asked when he looked up from screwing in the strike plate. "You look sick."

She felt sick. But not physically. "I'm okay," she assured her brother, reminding herself that she hadn't had any choice but to take the formula, she didn't have to feel good about it, she'd just had to do it.

"You're having another attack of the guilts, aren't you?" Gib guessed.

Blythe shrugged, but rather than answer she took the screwdriver out of her brother's hand. "I can do this. You put the other part on the door."

Gib didn't argue, stepping out of her way. As he picked up the remaining half of the dead-bolt assembly he glanced at the disarray of her living room. "Howard sure did make a mess of this place," he said quietly, as if reminding her that what they were doing was necessary.

"I know. I only had time to straighten out the bathroom when I came back from your place to change clothes."

"It's a good thing you had the formula with you, or he'd have found it. He didn't leave anything unturned."

Blythe didn't respond do that. Instead in her mind's eye she saw her old friend reduced to committing vandalism. Mild-mannered Howard tearing around her house like a madman, dumping drawers, flinging chair cushions, riffling through books....

"I'm glad you agreed to the bodyguard, Blythe," Gib went on, as if he were seeing the same picture. "I couldn't have rested, knowing you were by yourself tonight."

This time when the reference to Lee Farrell brought the image of the bodyguard to her mind it was a welcome escape from her thoughts of Howard. In fact it made her smile, and she seized the opportunity to give her brother a hard time again. "Who are you trying to kid? You just saw a bodyguard as another single man to throw at me."

Gib grinned at her. "No, you're wrong about that. I didn't even think about him being single, until I saw the guy and the way he couldn't take his eyes off you."

"Oh, right, he couldn't take his eyes off of me," she repeated sarcastically.

"You never know. It's always possible that it was fate that threw him at you."

When the doorbell rang a little before nine that night it startled Blythe into dropping the coffee can she was about to throw into the trash.

"Big, brave woman," she goaded herself. Half an hour earlier she'd nearly shoved Gib out of the house, after swearing that she was not afraid of being alone until the bodyguard came back.

Her heart pounding, she went to the living-room window and peeked through the side of the shade she'd pulled before Gib had left. If it was Howard standing just outside, she didn't want him to know she was home—if, of course, he hadn't already heard the clatter of the coffee can on the kitchen floor.

But it wasn't Howard. Lee Farrell was on the stoop, suitcase in hand.

Blythe took a deep breath and hurried to the front door. "Hi," she said as she unlocked the screen to let him in. "Sorry it took so long. I didn't want to open up until I was sure who you were."

He frowned slightly, causing two creases to appear between his pale blond eyebrows. "Are you alone? I thought your brother was going to stay until I got back."

"I made him leave. He still had paperwork to do tonight, and I didn't want to keep him any longer than I had to."

She closed the door and locked all three locks: the one in the knob, the dead bolt and the chain. When she turned around, Lee was checking them out over her shoulder.

"Looks like he did a good job on the door."

"He worked his way through college doing construction, so he's pretty handy." She wiped her palms down the thighs of the jeans she'd forbidden herself to change out of when the urge to fix herself up had hit just after Gib had left. Then she gestured to the wide-open space of the living room, which was separated from the kitchen by an oak dining table behind the blue plaid couch. "Sorry about the mess. I came home last night and found the place like this. I left right away and spent the night with my brother and his wife. This is the first chance I've had to start putting things back in order."

He looked over the room from end to end and she looked over him from top to bottom. He might not be a muscle-bound hulk, but he was no lightweight, either. His proportions were perfect; shoulders just broad enough, waist just narrow enough, hips...

Blythe skipped the hips and took in the thighs that bulged against the jeans he'd changed into.

"What happened?" he asked, nodding at the disarray.

"I think I was invaded by the Martian wrecking crew," she joked. Then she changed the subject. "I only have one bedroom, so I'm going to have to set you up on the couch. Luckily it's extralong and not too bad to sleep on." She headed for the kitchen. "Just put your suitcase down anywhere. After I get things straightened out you can use the coat closet.''

Behind the island counter Blythe started to sweep up a broken water glass. What was she supposed to do with this guy now that she had him here? she wondered. Should she try to keep up constant conversation? Ignore him and go on as if he were invisible? Sit him down in front of the TV? Offer him magazines?

''The place is small—just the bedroom down the hall to the left and the bath on the right. That's the laundry room over there.'' She nodded to the open doorway on the side wall. ''Go ahead and look around if you want, sort of get the lay of the land.''

The strong, silent type, she thought as he went down the hall without saying anything. Blythe lost track of her sweeping and leaned over the counter, watching him as he went. Okay, so he had nice buns. Extremely nice buns. It didn't do any harm to look.

Then he turned back and she straightened up in a hurry.

''Somebody really trashed this place,'' he said as he went into the living room and began putting cushions on the overstuffed sofa and matching chair. ''He or she must have been pretty desperate for whatever this valuable something is that I'm supposed to be protecting.''

''They sure turned the house upside down, all right,'' she agreed. It was clear he was curious about this situation, but Blythe had no intention of explaining anything to him.

''Do you have an idea who did it?'' he asked when she didn't offer any information.

''Oh, just a theory. Did you have dinner? Gib and I had pizza delivered, but there's some left. I can heat it for you if you're hungry. Or maybe you'd like a cup of tea?''

"I ate on the drive over, but thanks, anyway. And I'll pass on the tea, too."

Blythe swept the shattered glass into a dustpan and emptied the fragments into the trash. As she put the broom into the laundry room she couldn't resist glancing at Lee, who was setting her lamps back on the end tables. His help made her feel less as though she had a stranger in her house, and she appreciated that even more than the cleaning effort.

"Have you reported the break-in to the police?" he asked.

He got marks for persistence. "No, I haven't. And I should have told you before, I don't want them called— no matter what happens."

He shrugged. "Okay, I don't have a problem with that." He snatched up the newspapers that littered the floor, throwing her a reassuring smile when he caught her watching him.

She liked this guy, Blythe decided then. He was quiet and self-possessed.

"You know, it might help if you tell me what's going on, so I know what I'm on the lookout for."

She went back to work on the kitchen. "I'd rather not go into it all. The only thing you really need to know is that no matter what comes up—if anything even does— I want it handled very carefully, very gently."

"Carefully and gently," he repeated as if he didn't understand.

"*Very* carefully and gently," she confirmed.

His eyebrows arched. "Okay," he agreed as if things still didn't really make sense to him.

"And let's change the subject, if you don't mind."

He didn't say anything for a moment, and she had the feeling he was deciding whether or not to concede. Then he said, "Okay. New subject. Are you a Colorado native?"

"Born and raised," she answered. Feeling relieved, she began to empty the dishwasher, which was full of all the pots and pans and utensils that she'd taken off the floor earlier. "Are you?"

"Surprisingly enough, I am. It doesn't seem as if there's many of us still here."

"You're right. Almost everybody I meet is a transplant. Do you have family?"

"If you mean am I married—no. I haven't gotten around to that yet."

"Are you planning on it in the near future?" Gib would want to know these things.

"Not unless the right woman falls out of the sky tomorrow. What about you?"

"I came close to getting married once—or at least I thought I was close—but that was five years ago."

"And you haven't found anybody since?"

Now it was Blythe's turn to shrug. "I haven't been looking. Romantic involvements aren't high on my list of priorities."

"What is?"

She couldn't tell him that, so instead she joked, "Cleaning this mess is way up at the top." She changed the subject again. "Do you have brothers or sisters?"

He hesitated for a moment and Blythe wondered why. But then he said, "I have two brothers and a sister. What about you? Is there more than the brother who hired me?"

"No, there's just Gib and me. Are your parents still living?"

"Unfortunately not. Yours?"

"Both are still alive and well, thank God."

"Are they in Denver, too?"

"Technically."

"Technically?"

"Denver is where they pitstop between trips. They travel a lot. In fact they just left a few weeks ago to actually go around the world."

"Good for them."

Bending over to pick up debris had caused his hair to fall to his forehead. It made him look more relaxed, even more appealing. Blythe forced her eyes away and studied the silverware as she put it into the drawer. "Traveling is good for them," she went on, the thought of her parents giving her an old familiar twinge of envy. "They're very close—two people who genuinely enjoy each other, even after nearly forty years of marriage. I admire that. It seems as if Gib and his wife Gail have the same thing."

"You sound a little wishful."

That made her laugh. "Do I? I don't know why. I'm happy for them all, but I'm pretty content with my own life."

Everything in the kitchen was back in place. Blythe filled a bucket with sudsy water in the laundry room and brought it to mop the floor. As she did Lee replaced a wall clock that had left a shadow as evidence of where it went, upturned a footstool and righted the fireplace tools on the stone hearth in the corner.

"What do you do for a living?" he asked when she had finished mopping, emptied the bucket and was starting to work on the coat closet.

Had she thought he was the silent type? Obviously she'd been wrong. "I'm a research scientist."

"What kind of research?"

"Weight reduction," she said. She glanced expectantly at him over her shoulder. When he didn't say anything she smiled. "You get points for that."

He straightened up from plugging in a floor lamp. "For what?"

"For not being amazed. Most people I meet act like it's a big deal. Women as doctors and lawyers are commonplace now, but for some reason a woman biochemist still shocks the masses."

"Maybe it has something to do with the way you look."

Blythe moved toward him; he was replacing books on the shelves that lined an entire wall of the living room. She reached for the two he held and accidentally brushed his hand with her own. It struck her as odd that in that brief moment she became very aware of the structure of his hand. His skin felt tougher than hers, though not actually callused, and the bones were big and hard, the knuckles knobby. And he was so warm, almost hot, that the brief moment of contact was enough to impart a lingering heat that seeped all the way up her arm.

"You can put your stuff in the closet now if you want," she said, having a little difficulty in getting the words out. But once he moved away she found continuing their conversation easier. "So what is a scientist supposed to look like, anyway?"

He grinned at her as he went from his suitcase to the closet with shirts slung over his arm. "Plain, at best. Ugly as sin, at worst. But one way or the other they aren't supposed to have long, curly hair the color of devil's food cake or big, black eyes."

There was a compliment in his tone that both pleased and embarrassed her. And the fact that he had stopped before reaching the closet to look at her with that watchful gaze from his deep-set aquamarine eyes didn't help matters any. She kept shelving books as if she hadn't noticed.

"You don't have the profile of a research chemist, either," he went on, as if more to himself than to her.

"I save my hook nose with the wart on the end for Halloween," she joked. "That's okay, though. You don't fit my stereotype of a bodyguard, either."

"Yeah? Am I better or worse?" he inquired with a chuckle.

She liked men who could laugh at themselves and suddenly realized that if this were a date she'd be having a good time. "Better. I was afraid you might be some human gorilla."

"All body and no brains?"

Her embarrassment gone, Blythe grinned at him. "Something like that." He was easy to talk to. In fact he was easier to talk to than any man—except her brother—she'd ever met. If she had to have a bodyguard, wasn't it nice that she could enjoy his company? "The last thing I expected was..." What had she been going to say? That the last thing she'd expected was an extremely attractive man who was funny and personable and witty and charming? That wouldn't do. She settled on, "The last thing I expected was help cleaning up. Thanks. You cut the job in half."

"Sure." He shut his suitcase and slid it into the bottom of the closet. Closing the door, he retrieved a brown leather Dopp Kit from the dining table. "Can I stash this in the bathroom?"

She nodded as she put the last of the books away, then headed down the hall. "I'll make you a spot in the linen closet."

Her bathroom was so small that in order to open the closet door the bathroom door had to be shut. Together in the enclosed space Blythe again had that strange, exaggerated awareness of Lee. And it didn't help things that being so near to him gave her a whiff of his after-shave—a clean, piny scent. She tried to ignore it as she slid her makeup box, moisturizers and shampoo to one side of a shelf to make room for his shaving gear. But the moment he set his Dopp Kit next to her things, a rush of sensual feelings washed through her.

Now if that wasn't the dumbest thing she'd ever experienced! she thought. And over something so silly. It had been a tough week. Maybe things were catching up with her.

"While I'm in here, I might as well get the linens to set you up on the couch," she said, wondering at the weak sound of her voice.

She quickly took sheets from the bottom shelf, then reached for a blanket. That put her face close to where his shaving kit kept company with her toiletries and gave her an even stronger smell of the after-shave that must be inside the brown leather bag. She swallowed hard and turned her head away.

"All set?" he asked, taking the blanket out of her arms once she'd taken it down.

"I think so." She also thought she'd better put some distance between Lee and herself. And his shaving kit.

He led the way back to the living room. Blythe followed, paying close attention to the nape of his neck where his hair lay flat and straight against skin that was slightly sunburned. But as he lifted the back cushions off the plaid sofa and stacked them neatly in the chair she gained some control over her unruly eyes and stared at the floor until he was out of her way. Then she reformed the sofa seat into a bed. "There. That's not too bad," she said when she'd finished.

"It looks fine," he assured her.

Blythe took a deep breath, sighed and looked up at him with a smile that was hard to hold in place while she felt confusing emotions run amok inside her. "Well, I'm beat. I think I'll turn in," she informed him, aware that her voice was a little too bright. "I never have any trouble falling asleep, so if you want to watch television out here for awhile, feel free."

He nodded to the bookcase, and it almost seemed as if his expression was a little disappointed. "I think I'll borrow some reading material, instead. If you don't mind. We seem to have the same taste in novels."

"You're a mystery buff?"

"I love to figure out whodunit."

"Me, too." And she didn't really want to leave him to go to bed. "Well, good night."

"Good night."

It took some effort to drag her eyes away from his, but once Blythe had managed it she went to the back door, pushing hard to be sure it was tightly shut and checking the locks. Then she went into the laundry room and made sure the dowel was in the runner of the sliding window there.

"I just want to make sure everything is locked up tight," she explained a little sheepishly as she passed Lee again to check the front door.

Funny, she thought, but she hadn't been on edge about Howard the whole time Lee had been there. In fact she had barely thought about her old mentor. But remembering suddenly that he could be lurking outside brought all the tension back again.

"I'm really happy you're here," she told Lee when she turned to face him again. "Gib's idea to hire you was a good one."

A momentary frown pulled his brows together before he said, "I'm glad. Sleep well."

"You, too."

It was only as she closed her bedroom door behind her that Blythe realized she'd forgotten to ask why he'd become a bodyguard.

But wasn't it nice that she'd have another chance tomorrow?

Chapter Three

It was early when Lee woke up the next morning. He rolled onto his back, adjusted the blanket to cover his bare chest and cupped one hand behind his head. The couch was not as comfortable as his king-size bed at home, but it would do.

Wondering what time it was, he opened his eyes. There was a fanlight above the front door and through it he could see the cotton-candy-pink haze that dusted the sky. Barely dawn, he decided, closing his eyes again to go back to sleep.

But that wasn't easy when thoughts of the past evening instantly cropped up to leave him as troubled this morning as he'd been before falling asleep last night.

He had enjoyed Blythe's company too much. There was no doubt about it; he'd been so wrapped up in her that he'd had trouble keeping the reason he was here at the forefront of his thoughts.

No wonder Howard had been charmed into trusting her. Lee had to admit that since his aunt's phone call yesterday he'd wondered how his uncle could have been duped so completely by this woman. Now he knew. And it wasn't a reflection on Howard. Not by a long shot.

No, Blythe Coopersmith was a very likable lady. She had an air about her that made her seem open and honest and wholesome. That made her seem like the girl next door grown up to be a beautiful woman. It was a powerful combination. And it was hard to see through. In fact, if Lee didn't know better, he'd swear she was incapable of doing what she had done to Howard.

But of course he did know better. He knew that what he had enjoyed last night was only an image she presented. Likable, open, honest, wholesome girls next door didn't pirate someone else's discovery.

She was good at keeping up the front, though. Lee had to give her that. And she had the nervous act down pat. It was so subtle it was almost believable—the barely audible tremors in her voice that she seemed to be trying to camouflage, checking the doors and windows as if she really was on edge, when in truth she just didn't want to give Howard easy access. She'd even gone so far as to tell Lee she was glad he was here. As if she really thought she was in some kind of danger. From Howard? *Come off it, lady.*

Too bad she was dealing with someone who knew the truth, Lee thought. Howard might be angry. He might even be furious enough to break a window and come into her house when she wasn't here, but he'd never hurt a fly, no matter how mad he was. And Blythe had to know that.

You're playing to the wrong audience, Coopersmith.

Lee pulled his shoulders back until he heard one of them crack. Then he dug them deeper into the sofa cushion and turned his head to one side, hoping that a change of position would get him a little more sleep, after all.

There was only one problem.

Blythe had a distinctive scent. Lee didn't think it came from perfume. Maybe it was her shampoo or lotion or that powder she kept on the shelf in the bathroom. Whatever it was, it was like a mixture of wildflowers and grasses, but light enough to seem as natural as she did. And the couch smelled faintly of it.

How could something so mild have such a strong effect? One whiff of it did weird things to him. Last night it had made him incapable of concentrating on the book he'd chosen from her shelves. Both then and now it left the sound of her laughter in his ears. It made him remember that when she laughed, those black eyes of hers grew moist and glimmered. It made him curious to know if her skin was as soft as it looked. It made him wonder what she tasted like. All over. It made him remember how sorry he'd been to have her leave him to go to bed. And just one hint of that smell that was so uniquely hers made him want to bury his face in that mane of shiny hair....

Damn.

Lee turned his head the other way.

Remember what she did.

Instead he thought what an uncommon rapport they had with each other. How easy it was to spend time with her! He couldn't help remembering that he found her interesting, that he liked talking to her. That spending time with her could actually make him forget she'd stolen Howard's formula, make him forget both his loyalties to his uncle and how little tolerance Lee himself had for one person betraying another.

But she did steal Howard's formula, he told himself sternly. And she still had it, even though Howard had torn her house apart looking for it.

The renewal of his anger made him feel better.

He hadn't completely lost sight of why he was here, he reassured himself. After all, he'd seen through her concern that he should handle carefully anything that might come up; her concern stemmed more from her guilty conscience than from worrying over Howard.

A wolf in sheep's clothing—that was what Ms. Blythe Coopersmith was, he thought as he finally slipped back toward sleep. And he wasn't going to forget it. Any more than he was going to let himself like her.

The formula for EASY was not in the bathroom. By the time Lee finished his shower later that morning he was sure of it, because he'd searched every inch of every shelf, cupboard and drawer. He'd even checked inside boxes and bags he had no business getting into. But the formula wasn't there.

Knowing he'd already spent an overly long time in the bathroom, he quickly pulled on a black mock turtleneck T-shirt and jeans, combed his wet hair and walked out.

"Come on, Jackson Labs can make me a better offer than that," he heard Blythe cajole as he went into the living room.

Hoping it would seem as if he weren't eavesdropping, he opened the closet door and straightened everything hanging there, listening to her conversation all the while. From Blythe's half of the call it was clear that she was discussing money, apparently with someone she knew well enough to tease.

Listening to her brought a new sense of urgency to Lee. It was only logical that she'd try to pass the formula on as quickly as she could; but it hadn't occurred to him that she would have already had time to contact interested potential buyers.

Then he heard her say, "Well, you see what you can do for me and let me know," just before she hung up.

Lee stepped out of the closet and went to the island counter where Blythe met him with a small pot of coffee. Standing just around the corner from him she smiled, for all the world as innocent as an angel in her sky-blue polo shirt and jeans, her hair braided down her back.

"Good morning," she said as if she were glad to see him. "I figured since you wouldn't have tea last night that you were probably a coffee drinker, so I made a pot."

"Thanks," he answered, wondering if she'd caught the clipped tone of voice that had slipped away from him. "You were right. I hate tea." He leaned over to sniff the steam as she poured. "But this smells great."

She slid his mug across the butcher-block top and curled her hands around one of her own. "I hate coffee," she informed him, wrinkling her nose in an appealing way that Lee tried to ignore.

He took a sip, then pointed his chin at the wall phone beside the back door. "Sorry I came out in the middle of your call. And I'm sorry I overheard some it it, but it's hard not to with things so close around here."

"It's okay. If it had been a top secret call I would have used the phone in my bedroom—which, by the way, you're welcome to if you need some privacy."

"Thanks." He drank his coffee again. "I'd say you were talking to a boyfriend except for the mention of money."

"Nope, it was a business call." She sipped her tea and only those big black eyes of hers, sparkling and wide, were visible over the cup. Lee dragged his gaze down to her hand; her fingers were long and delicate, the nails pink and perfect. Again he forced his eyes away, concentrating on the steam wafting up from his mug instead.

"You know," he mused, "I've been thinking about things, putting two and two together to try to figure out what's going on around here."

"What kind of things?"

He shrugged. "Well, part of why I'm here is to protect something valuable and you're a research scientist. Could it be that I'm here to keep some great discovery from being stolen? And then there's that phone call. I can't help wondering if it had something to do with selling that discovery."

"Ah, you are a mystery buff, aren't you?" she asked through narrowed eyes that only played at being stern.

"It's partly from that," he conceded. "And partly that the bodyguard in me wants to know what I'm protecting. I can understand you're being secretive about it, but to do my job well I really do need not to be kept in the dark."

She seemed to think about that. "You're probably right," she agreed after a moment. Then she hesitated again before saying a little reluctantly, "There is a formula involved in this."

Lee reminded himself that he wasn't supposed to know anything about EASY and tried to imagine what questions a real, uninformed bodyguard would ask. "A formula for what?"

"Weight reduction."

"And I'm here to protect it from someone until you can market it?"

With her cup between both hands she put her elbows on the butcher-block countertop and leaned on them. Lee took a drink of coffee to swallow back the effort it was taking him not to look at her rear end, which was jutting out.

"The formula is a long way from the marketing stage," she said. "Nothing like this can be offered to the public without extensive animal and human testing and approval by the FDA. Besides, marketing isn't my field, even if the formula was ready for that. When the time comes, the pharmaceutical company that's licensed it will handle manufacturing and sales."

"Then you were discussing the licensing."

"Do you want some cereal? I'm not much of a breakfast eater but I do have some cornflakes."

"Cornflakes are fine," he said, wondering if she was purposely avoiding his question.

He watched her stretch up for the cereal box on a high shelf of a cupboard and this time he lost the battle to keep his gaze from straying to her derriere. Not too wide, not too flat. Just about enough to fit in his hands.

Lee closed his eyes and ran an index finger around the inside of the turtleneck that suddenly seemed too tight.

Blythe brought the makings of his breakfast back to the counter. She still didn't seem inclined to answer his question and, not wanting to seem too preoccupied with the formula, he decided to play dumb instead. "So let me see if I understand this. You came up with a formula for some sort of a diet aid. I assume it's valuable. But until you finish testing it and get the FDA's approval, it's fair game for anyone who gets their hands on it—like whoever it was who broke the glass out of your front door. So you hired a bodyguard to protect it."

She fixed his cereal, not looking up as she replied, "Something like that."

"There must be other ways to safeguard a discovery. I've never been called on to do this before," he said, sounding as innocent as she looked.

"No, I don't think bodyguards are the norm," she admitted. "There's a way that's a lot more practical. When a person gets an idea they think is original they write it down on a piece of paper, along with the date, and have it witnessed. Then they send it to themselves by registered mail and put it somewhere safe—like in a safety deposit box. Then if anyone else files for a patent on the same thing or claims it, you go to court. The postmark proves the date, and the letter is opened in front of the judge to confirm the contents. The right to patent and market the idea—or an invention or a discovery—goes to the person who came up with it first." She put the bowl of cereal in front of him.

"But you didn't send yourself a registered letter?"

"There wasn't one sent, no. Anyway, this particular formula isn't actually finished yet, so at the moment that's what I'm concentrating on."

Lee's spoon stopped halfway to his mouth. What did she mean, the formula wasn't actually finished? Howard already had an offer from Healthco Labs to license and manufacture it and had asked that the next two stages in the process be put into motion. Then it dawned on Lee that she was protecting both the formula and herself from him. Obviously she wanted him to think it was unfinished, so he wouldn't get any ideas about pulling on her what she had pulled on Howard.

"Well." She stood up and took her cup to the dishwasher. "I have to get to work. I'm using the laundry room as a lab."

But instead of going into the small adjoining space she headed for the front door. Opening it she said, "There you are, my little babies. Your Uncle Gib said he'd have you brought back this morning." She stepped outside.

Cats? Lee wondered. Or maybe puppies?

She came back a few seconds later carrying a wire cage at eye level as she crooned to its occupants.

"Rats?" Lee inquired, too surprised to keep distaste out of his voice.

Blythe looked at him from around the side of the cage. "Mice," she corrected. "Maude and Hershel. I was at the pet store buying them the night before last when the Martian wrecking crew tore my house apart. I forgot to bring them back from Gib's yesterday, so he promised to have someone leave them on the porch before I got up today."

Lee took a step back as she brought them nearer.

She laughed. "You should see the look on your face. They're only little white mice." She swung the cage toward him and Lee went back two more paces. "I take it you don't like mice?" she asked, laughing again.

He held up his hands, warding her off with his palms outward. "You have snakes you want taken care of, I'm your man. Spiders, bees, moths, bugs of any kind, I'd be happy to deal with them. But I draw the line at rats."

"Mice. Just look at these cute little pink tails and those wiggling pointed noses."

"You look. I don't want anything to do with them."

She grinned at him as if she were delighted. "You're not kidding, are you? You're really afraid of mice?"

"I'm not afraid of them. I just don't like them."

Her grin got even wider. "Right." She set the cage on the counter as far away from him as possible and took four cookies out of the same cupboard the cereal had been in. As she broke them into smaller pieces she said, "They won't hurt you, you know."

He made a face. "I didn't say they would. They're just..." He struggled to find a word bad enough and settled on, "gross."

She put the cookies into the small pan attached to two of the cage's bars, then ran an index finger down the spine of one of the furry white rodents. "Don't listen to him, guys. He doesn't know what he's talking about. You're beautiful."

"They can have my cereal if they want it," he offered. "I think I've lost my appetite."

"Okay, I get the hint. I'll take them in the laundry room with me. But you might like them if you get to know them."

"I sincerely doubt it."

She took the cage off the counter, then paused to look him up and down. "Isn't it always the way—big lions afraid of little mice?" she goaded, just before going into the laundry room and closing the door.

It was the sound of the lock clicking that made Lee remember; her rats weren't what he should be nervous about.

The formula for EASY. Was she really fiddling with it? Why would she? But why would she lock herself in that laundry room if she wasn't doing something with the formula?

This particular twist didn't make sense, and since he'd yet to call Howard and let him know what was going on, Lee decided it was time to talk to his uncle. But he didn't want to do it here, where there was any chance of Blythe overhearing.

He knocked on the laundry room door.

"Sorry, but Maude and Hershel can't come out to play," she called.

"I thought I'd run to the grocery store and pick up some of my own brand of coffee. Think you'll be all right if I make a quick trip?"

"Sure, as long as everything is locked. There's an extra key on the pegboard next to the door. Go ahead and take it with you so you can let yourself back in."

"Do you need anything?"

"No, but thanks for asking."

For a moment Lee stayed where he was, struck again by how nice she sounded. Then he forced that notion out of his head. Coopersmith the Carnivore. Coopersmith the Carnivore. Why was it so hard to remember?

At the grocery store Lee made quick work of picking up his coffee, some cream and a package of bagels. Then he went to the pay phone near the entrance and dialed his uncle's number.

"Howard? It's me."

"Bucky! Where have you been? I must've called your house a million times since last night and all I get is that damn machine."

In his mind Lee could see his tall, lanky uncle absentmindedly running a bony hand through his salt-and-pepper-gray hair and making it stand on end the way he did when he was agitated. "Did Aggie tell you I was going to see Blythe Coopersmith for you?"

"That's why I've been trying to get you. I wanted to know what happened. Did you get her to give back the formula?"

"Not exactly." Someone came up to use the pay phone beside Lee's. He turned his back to the woman and lowered his voice. Anybody who overheard this was bound to think he was crazy. "I went over to her place late yesterday afternoon," he began, explaining the events that had led to his pretending to be Blythe's bodyguard.

"Then you're there? In her house? Good for you, Bucky!" Howard's usually soft voice was raised and he was talking so fast Lee couldn't get a word in edgewise. Until his uncle shouted, "I'll be right over!"

"Hold on. Howard, listen to me."

"We can talk when I get there. You sit on Blythe if you have to. Just don't let her out of your sight."

"Wait, Howard." Lee knew he'd raised his own voice louder than he'd meant to. And even then he wasn't sure he'd gotten through to his uncle.

"What?" Howard barked back.

Surprised by the tone, Lee patiently replied, "Just hold your horses and listen to me. Carefully. Are you there?"

"Yes, I'm here." Howard's tone was clipped.

"Good. In the first place I'm at a pay phone at the moment, I'm not at her house. In the second place, I told you she doesn't know who I am. She thinks I'm staying with her to *keep* you from getting to her. All you could do if I let you see her is demand that she hand EASY over to you—and blow my cover in the process. She didn't pirate your work just to give it up for the asking, and then I'd be locked out the same way you've been. Just stay where you are and let me handle this. I'll gain her trust, get my hands on the formula and bring it back to you."

"No, dammit! EASY is mine! She doesn't have any business keeping it from me and I'm going to take it back!"

Lee could hear his aunt's voice in the background telling Howard to calm down. Lee tried reasoning with him. "Of course EASY is yours, and she doesn't have any business keeping it from you. But you've already tried to take it back and it hasn't worked, has it? I thought you didn't want to make a big deal out of this? I thought that was why you didn't want the police called? If I hang around long enough to get my hands on the formula and walk out the front door with it the way she did, we'll accomplish just that."

"By God, she should have to face me with what she's done. I should be able to tell her what I think of her turning on me like this!" Howard shouted.

"You can do that after I've put the formula safely in your hands. To act prematurely might cost you getting EASY back at all. Is that what you want?"

"No," his uncle growled. "But I'm not waiting around forever, either."

Lee heard his aunt say, "Don't speak to him like that. He's on our side."

"You won't have to wait around forever," Lee assured him. "I'm living with her, for crying out loud, in a house the size of my garage. There can't be that many places for her to hide the damn thing, so it can't take me too long to find it. You just need to be patient."

"You want me to sit on my butt until she sells EASY out from under me?" Howard grumbled.

"I'm not going to let her sell it out from under anyone." That reminded Lee of something else. "You did say the formula was finished, didn't you?"

"Of course it's finished. That's why she took it. She waited until I'd done all the work—six years of it—and then she stole it from me."

Again Lee heard his aunt's voice in the background, chastising Howard for this show of temper. Then Howard said angrily, "Your aunt wants to talk to you."

Aggie came on before Lee could say anything else. "I'm sorry, Lee," she said on the gust of a sigh. "This whole thing has your uncle so upset he isn't himself."

"I didn't realize just how upset he was until now."

"That's why I wanted you to handle this. I've never seen him this way, and to tell you the truth I'm not sure what he might do. I couldn't believe he actually broke that woman's window and went into her house."

"EASY is the major accomplishment of his career so far. Another man probably would have done worse to her by now."

"Well, he's in a bad way. He isn't sleeping, he's hardly eating. He can't think about anything else."

"Just try to reassure him that I'll take care of it," Lee said, going on to briefly explain to his aunt what he was doing. "But you have to keep Howard from coming to her house," he finished. "She was willing to hire a bodyguard before. If she gets wind of who I am there's no telling what she'll do to keep us from getting EASY back."

"I'll do everything I can," Aggie assured him.

But in his aunt's voice Lee heard her uncertainty that anything she did would have an effect on Howard in his present state of mind.

Having a bodyguard was a good idea, but maybe having Lee as that bodyguard wasn't such a great one, Blythe thought as she stared out the window of her laundry room.

Spread on the top of the washer and dryer were pages and pages of barely legible notes scrawled in Howard's hand. After a week of going through them she had barely managed to decipher half of her old friend's work. And though it was nearly five o'clock she'd made less head-way today than on any day so far.

She just plain hadn't been able to concentrate.

It was Lee's fault.

Never in her life had she been as distracted from her work as she had been today. No matter what she'd tried, she couldn't get away from mental images of her body-guard and wanting to be out in the living room talking to him.

It really was ridiculous. Romantic daydreaming was not her style.

She got down off the bar stool she was sitting on and bent way over, dangling her arms, so her fingertips brushed the floor and her head swayed back and forth. Maybe a little blood to her brain would help.

When she could feel her face flushed she straightened up, stretched to the ceiling and breathed deeply.

Lee Farrell was only a man, after all. He wasn't any-thing special enough to take her mind off the most im-portant research work she'd ever done.

Well, maybe he was a little special, she admitted to herself when she sat down on the stool again, looked at a page of Howard's notes and saw instead the mental image of Lee's biceps bulging from the short sleeves of that black T-shirt he was wearing today.

Or maybe she was just hungry, she thought hopefully. After all, she'd skipped lunch and hadn't had anything but coffee and three cookies for breakfast. Distracting thoughts and mental pictures of Lee were more likely just her mind's answer to nothing but caffeine and sugar in her bloodstream.

Anyway, it was only an hour or so before she usually quit work for the day.

She gathered the papers into a pile, lifted her shirt and stuffed them halfway down her jeans before pulling the sky-blue knit over the top half.

"Don't look at me like that, Maude," she whispered to the mouse poking her nose through the bars of the cage. "This may look ridiculous, but you never know who you can trust. There's no sense risking that even a hired bodyguard might get an idea of where I'm taking these notes to hide them."

She picked up the cage, unlocked the door and went into the kitchen.

"The scientist surfaces," Lee greeted her. "I was beginning to wonder if you were ever coming up for air."

"There's air in the laundry room."

"There must be food, too, or else you would have taken my offer to make you lunch."

"No, I just wasn't hungry then. But I am now. Do you like beef Stroganoff?"

"Sure." He made a face and nodded toward the mouse cage. "Unless you make it with those, in which case I'll pass."

Blythe wrapped an arm protectively around the cage. "Watch what you say. Hershel is very sensitive. I'm just going to feed them and put them away for the night. Then I'll clean up and cook."

Maude and Hershel had a smorgasbord of bread, cheese, peanut butter, cashews, cookies and ice cream before being retired to the laundry room. Then Blythe headed for her bedroom.

There were ink stains on her shirt, so she changed into a high-necked plaid blouse, refusing to wonder why she had chosen something she usually saved to wear for good. She hid the formula in the bathroom, then freshened her blush and put on a little pale lipstick. Gloss was what she ordinarily wore, but the blouse seemed to call for more. Then she took her hair out of its braid, brushed it and caught it at the nape of her neck with an elastic ruffle.

"What can I do to help?" Lee asked when she went into the kitchen to start dinner.

"Can you chop onions without cutting yourself?"

"Try me," he challenged.

Don't tempt me. "Okay, then get them out of the bin in the refrigerator. The knives are in that drawer next to the dishwasher and the cutting board is in the cupboard up above."

Blythe watched to make sure he found what he needed. When he went to work on the countertop beside the sink she turned to the stove that made the kitchen an L shape. They were standing rear cheek to rear cheek as Blythe made the sauce.

"So tell me, where are you keeping this formula I'm supposed to be guarding?" he asked.

She laughed at the innocence that unsubtly hid his curiosity. "I'll never tell. A woman has to have some mystery to her."

"I hardly know you. That makes you a complete mystery to me. But how am I supposed to protect something when I don't even know where it is?"

"If you can't find it, then neither can anybody else," she reasoned. "Your job is to keep the field clear. I'll take care of the formula."

"You sound pretty sure of yourself."

Blythe shrugged. "I think it's safe enough," she said with finality, letting the sizzle of sautéing meat speak for her for a moment. "I'm about ready for the onions. Think you can grab the sliced mushrooms out of the fridge on your way? I need them, too."

He did, adding both the mushrooms and the onions to her frying pan when she told him to.

"Have you always worked alone in your laundry room?" he asked, leaning against the edge of the counter and crossing his arms over his chest.

"Never before this past week. I was lucky to get a job in the University of Colorado's research department when I finished graduate school. I stayed there for four years, working as an assistant to Nicholas Springer. You may have heard of him—he invented a broad-spectrum antibiotic that's effective on some forms of viral infections. It made quite a splash. There were articles in three different national magazines."

"Did he invent it while you were working with him?"

"The exact moment," she said proudly.

"But he came up with it, not you?"

She laughed at that idea. "I was just a rookie. He was brilliant."

"Surely you made some contribution?"

Why did that sound like a challenge? Blythe shook her head. "Very little. It was his idea and his discovery. I was lucky to be working with him on it. I learned a lot from him." She could feel Lee's eyes on her and glanced at him, finding his expression curious. "What? Do I have flour on my nose or something?"

He just shook his head. "You said you worked there for four years. Where did you go after that?"

"Grab some plates out of that cupboard next to the refrigerator, will you?" she instructed first, putting the finished Stroganoff into a serving bowl and taking that, napkins and silverware to the table as she answered his question. "I went on to learn what a mistake it is to mix business with personal life," she said as she returned to the kitchen for glasses of ice water. "That took two years and then I went to work with a man who had been one of my professors and the head of research at CU. He'd left just after I did to start his own independent group and he took me in with him when things fell apart for me."

Lee held her chair out for her, then took the one across the table for himself as she served him first. "How did things fall apart?" he asked.

"It's not important anymore," she told him. "What about you? I've been dying to know how you got to be a bodyguard."

He had to finish chewing and swallowing. Then he took a drink of water, too, and pointed a curved index finger at his plate. "This is great stuff," he said to avoid answering.

"Thanks." Blythe ate her own food, watching him take another bite of his, still without addressing her question. "Is it a deep, dark secret?"

His eyebrows shot up. "What?"

"How you got to be a bodyguard."

He shrugged. "I just sort of fell into it," he said vaguely. "What about you? How did you decide to be a research scientist?"

Was he embarrassed about what he did for a living? she wondered. "I got hooked on chemistry from a toy set of Gib's when I was a kid. I know it sounds a little strange, but science just got more and more interesting with every class I took and one thing led to another, I guess."

"And weight research? How did you go from working with somebody who was dealing with antibiotics to that?"

"It was personal, actually. I've fought the battle of the bulge since I was twelve."

He leaned around the corner of the table and took a closer look. "I don't believe that."

"Oh, it's true," she said, pushing away the last of her Stroganoff. "I love food, and it loves me so much it likes to hang on forever."

"I don't know where," he said sincerely as he took a second helping of the sauce-laden meat and mushrooms.

She eyed his plate. "And it always seemed so unfair that some people can eat as much as they want and never put on a pound. I decided to see if I could find an equalizer."

He watched his fork. "And now you have," he said, slightly under his breath..

Blythe had run into men who were threatened by her education and accomplishments but hadn't thought Lee was one of them. Somehow she still didn't believe he was. Nonetheless, she didn't understand that last comment. "Did you go to college?" she asked, as if changing the subject.

He nodded, pushing his plate away now that it was empty. "Stanford."

"What did you major in?"

"Engineering."

"Didn't you like it once you graduated?"

He stood up and piled the dirty dishes in the nearly empty serving bowl, taking everything to the sink. "I liked it well enough," he allowed as he began to rinse plates and put them into the dishwasher.

Blythe brought their glasses and went back with a sponge to wipe off the table. "But not well enough to keep at it?"

"No," he answered simply.

She sensed withdrawal on his part and wondered why he didn't want to talk about this. "Doing what you do must be more exciting," she suggested.

With the dishes all in the machine he dried his hands and turned a wicked smile on her, leaning with one hand on the rim of the sink. "I sat here and read all afternoon, not much excitement in that."

"I'm just a boring case."

Again his gaze raked her from top to bottom and back again. "Boring is one thing you're not," he said, maintaining that smile.

Those aquamarine eyes of his locked on hers, and Blythe felt the pull of them as if they were tractor beams. Forcing herself to break their hold, she took the sponge back to the sink to rinse it and bent to put it into a holder on the inside of the cupboard door. She hadn't realized how close by Lee was until she caught a glimpse of the zipper on his jeans out of the corner of her eye, a scant few inches away. Her ears started to ring and she shot back up quickly.

"I don't know, I think I'm a pretty unexciting person," she observed in an effort to recover the aplomb she'd lost somewhere on the way up. But she succeeded only in giving herself away when her voice came out high and thin.

"There's one thing I can say for sure," he answered and Blythe realized his voice had changed, too, reaching deeper, quieter, more intimate levels. "I haven't been bored by you for one second that we've been together."

Those incredible eyes of his met and held hers. Was she imagining it, or was he moving closer?

She was suddenly aware of the creases between his brows, the bare hint of his beard, the lines bracketing his mouth and the soft salmon color of his lips.

No doubt about it, he was coming nearer.

A little late, she realized that he was about to kiss her. Two things happened—the ringing in her ears grew louder and she remembered that they were two strangers living in very close quarters—it was not wise to get carried away.

Blythe drew back, and at the first hint of her retreat, Lee straightened away from her.

"I'll show you how dull I am," she told him with some difficulty, wanting to fill the awkward moment with sound. "The highlight of this day is going to be the long, hot bubble bath I'm about to take."

For a moment his gaze stayed locked with hers. Then he nodded and she wondered if he was agreeing with her idea to take a bath, or with her preventing what had been developing between them before it got out of hand.

"Enjoy it," he replied. "I think I'll get a little air."

She started to point out that the evenings were still too cool for comfort, then realized the cold spring air was probably what he wanted. It was certainly what *she* needed, in spite of her claim to be heading for a steamy soak. Instead she said, "I'll probably just go on to bed afterward, so I'll say good night now."

He nodded again; there was a wealth of understanding in the simple gesture. "See you in the morning," he said.

Blythe made a quick retreat down the hall, hearing the back-door screen bang shut at about the same time she closed the bathroom door. Forgetting why she'd gone there in the first place, she turned on the cold water and leaned over the sink to splash her face with it.

If only it would rinse away the thought of that kiss that might have been.

But there it was in her mind: his lips closing the distance to hers, warm and smooth and just the slightest bit moist....

Blythe threw even more water onto her face.

Disappointment was alive inside her and she couldn't get rid of it.

The man was a stranger, she reminded herself.

It didn't seem to matter.

Stranger or not, she felt as comfortable with him as if she'd known him forever. He was easy to talk to. He was intelligent. He was so much more than just an attractive hunk of well-built masculinity.

Then it dawned on her.

In some ways Lee reminded her of Howard.

Not that she had ever had any romantic inclinations toward her mentor. But maybe that was where the familiarity and the comfort she felt with Lee came in. His rapt interest in what she had to say, his easy manner, his humor, were similar to those same qualities in Howard. Qualities she'd appreciated in her friendship with the older man.

The problem was that what she was feeling for Lee was more than friendship. Hotter than friendship. And she didn't want that to happen.

She turned off the water in the sink and ran a nearly cold bath, dropping her clothes into a heap and sitting down in the tub as if she were on fire.

If she could avoid this heat that seemed to be developing between them it would be nice to have Lee as Howard's replacement in the friendship department, she thought. It would help to fill the gap.

But could she do it? Could she ignore the heat and simply concentrate on starting a friendship?

Of course she could. After all, this was just a matter of hormones, and surely she could control that. She could do anything she put her mind to.

If only she could stop wondering what it would have been like if she had let him kiss her.

That was easier said than done.

Chapter Four

It was late when Lee woke up the next morning. Blythe's bedroom door was still closed, so he knew she'd overslept, too. Had she had as bad a night as he'd had? he wondered as he swung his legs to the floor and sat on the edge of his makeshift bed. More importantly, if she hadn't been asleep, had she heard him?

Probably not, he decided, or she would have come out and asked what he was doing.

How would he have explained that he was searching through her house for the formula she'd pirated? Not that he had anything to show for his efforts.

The first place he'd checked, once he'd judged she'd fallen asleep, was the laundry room. He'd covered every square inch of the small space that housed only a washer, a dryer, a bar stool, a rough gray washtub, a shelf with the necessary laundry products, and Maude and Hershel.

He had searched inside the appliances, behind them, under them, had opened every bottle and box until he'd made sure EASY wasn't there. He'd even gritted his teeth and checked under the newspapers that lined the bottom of the mouse cage and lifted the whole thing to see if the formula was attached to the bottom. It hadn't been.

Then Lee had scoured the kitchen in case Blythe had hidden the papers there while his back was turned. That had been a bigger job. Inside every cupboard, every container, every jar, every cannister, even everything in the refrigerator. All he'd found was the most incredible stockpile of chocolate in every form he'd ever seen.

Even when he'd finished with the kitchen, he hadn't been able to rest without going over the bath and living rooms again, just to be sure.

Lee scratched his night's growth of beard, realizing that unless Blythe was carrying the formula around with her all the time the only place left to search was her bedroom.

How was he going to get into her room when she wasn't using it, when the formula wasn't with her in the laundry room, or when she wasn't around to wonder why he was going through her drawers?

Lee ran his hands through his hair. He'd just have to bide his time, that was all. Or hope he could win her trust enough for her to let him know where EASY was.

He checked to make sure her door was still closed, then went to the telephone in the kitchen and dialed. While he listened to the ring he unlocked the back door and slipped out onto the redwood deck.

"Hi. Sally, it's me. Is Chad around?"

The secretary he and Chad shared asked him to hang on. While he waited Lee stretched the phone cord far enough to watch Blythe's bedroom door through the greenhouse window over the kitchen sink.

"I'm here," Chad said when he came onto the line.

"Morning."

"Not for much longer. You sound as if you just got out of bed."

"I did."

"Rough night? Or has the enemy won you over to her side?" his friend goaded sarcastically.

Lee did a little internal squirming but thought he managed to keep it out of his voice. "I was awake until four this morning searching the house."

"Did you come up with anything?"

"Eleven variations of chocolate candy, four of chocolate cookies and two of ice cream."

"And beyond knowing that she's not a health-food addict?"

"Nothing," Lee complained. "What about you? Did you talk to your old lab assistant girlfriend?"

"Sorry. I called and she's out of town until tonight or tomorrow."

"Damn."

"I've been thinking about it, though, and I seem to recall Virginia singing a lot of praises for our lady scientist. It sticks in my mind, because I was struck by her saying such glowing things, when the gossip could easily have paved the way for back stabbing. As I recall, Virginia agreed with Howard about it being hard to believe that Coopersmith had done what gossip said she did. Seems to me words like innovative, imaginative and cooperative came up. If I'm remembering this right, maybe Howard wasn't the only person Coopersmith did a snow job on."

His uncle definitely wasn't the only person, Lee reflected. "Innovative, imaginative and cooperative," he repeated. Why were those characteristics easier to accept about Blythe than the bad ones?

"You better watch this woman," Chad warned. "She must be some piece of work."

"She's good at hiding any flaws she might have," Lee conceded.

There was silence on the line for a moment. "You aren't starting to doubt that she did what she did, are you?" Chad inquired carefully.

That was just what made this whole thing so confusing—there wasn't a doubt in Lee's mind that Blythe had taken the formula. "No, I'm not," he answered his friend.

"Is she getting to you, anyway?"

Chad knew him too well. Lee jammed a hand through his hair again, pulling his head back as he did so and staring at the clear blue sky. "I'd just like to find the damn formula and get out of here," was all he'd admit to. "I'd better get off before she comes out and I have to explain this call."

"Okay. I left a message for Virginia to contact me as soon as she gets in. I said it was an emergency, so hopefully I'll hear from her sometime between tonight and tomorrow. Check back."

"I will."

Lee took a deep breath and glanced through the kitchen window. Blythe's door was still shut. He slipped back into the house and hung up the phone, but his friend's words were still ringing in his ears.

Was Blythe getting to him?

He could hardly deny it when he'd almost kissed her last night. And that wasn't even the worst of it. Afterward he'd actually regretted not doing it. Even now he couldn't honestly say that if he had the opportunity again he wouldn't take advantage of it.

Maybe being a traitor was contagious.

Disgusted with himself, he grabbed clean clothes and headed for the shower.

If only he could find her bad side, he thought along the way. If only he could see it for himself. Even just a hint of it. Something that showed him what there was at her core that could allow her to stab a man like Howard in the back. Something that would show him that what was attracting him was only a false front.

Then, maybe, he could stop himself getting to like her more and more. Then, maybe, he wouldn't enjoy her company quite so much, wouldn't be needing to take this cold shower to cool down from wanting last night's kiss to have not only started but gone further.

Maybe.

A dream finally woke Blythe—a nightmare that jolted her out of sleep and left her perspiring, while the images and feelings lingered.

In the dream Howard was her enemy. Howard hated her. Howard wanted to hurt her.

The burden of her actions over the past week weighed Blythe down. She opened her eyes and looked at the clock on her night table. After eleven. She couldn't believe it was so late. But even the sunshine diffused through her curtains, bathing her room in a yellow glow, didn't let her escape the emotions that had chased her out of her dream, feelings that made knowing what she was putting her old friend through hard to bear.

I'm sorry, Howard. I'm sorry I had to do it. If there had been any other option, I would have taken it.

But the deed was done and there was no going back. Even if she had it to do over again she knew she wouldn't change anything.

Too bad she couldn't say the same thing about the kiss that might have been. The one that had kept her awake most of the night. If she had that to do over again...

No, don't think about that, she told herself.

Blythe got out of bed and shrugged into her robe. That simple act was all it took to revive those thoughts. How many times last night had she sneaked out from under her covers and put on this same robe just this way, intending to go into that living room and spend more time with her bodyguard in the hope that one thing would lead to another and she might get a taste of that kiss, after all?

Too many times. Up and down. Up and down. It had been the best aerobic exercise she'd had in years.

But ultimately she hadn't gone through with it. Ultimately reason had prevailed.

So had disappointment.

Now she swore to herself that she was going to keep the skids on this attraction. In the last week she'd complicated her life as much as she could handle for the moment, and the fact that the kiss hadn't actually happened was like a second chance to keep this relationship with Lee simple. She meant to make the best of that second chance.

But if there were to be another time, another place, other circumstances?

At another time, in another place, under other circumstances, Blythe thought, she just might have gone ahead and let Lee kiss her.

And she'd have kissed him back.

Boy, would she have kissed him back!

* * *

Blythe didn't feel much better after she had showered and dressed in her most comfortable jeans and a bright flowered Henley T-shirt. She made her bed, straightened her room and headed for the kitchen.

Lee was halfway down her extended front yard getting the newspaper. It didn't surprise her to know he had probably slept as late as she had. After all, she'd heard him moving around out here the whole time she'd been awake. Had the missed kiss been on his mind, too?

His coffee was already perking, so Blythe took the teapot off the stove and went to the sink. She removed the lid, positioned the pot under the faucet and turned the spigot. But instead of water coming out there was a terrible groan in the pipes, then a loud bang, followed by a geyser that blew open the cupboard door beside her.

Blythe jumped away, staring at what looked like the opening of a fire hydrant flooding her kitchen. She closed the spigot but nothing happened.

"Where's the main water shutoff?" Lee asked as he rushed from the doorway.

Of course. "It's in the laundry room," Blythe said as she headed there. Within minutes the geyser stopped and she went back into the kitchen, to find Lee hunkered down on his wet-tennis-shoe-clad feet, his head stuck inside the cupboard.

"What's the problem?" she asked, wading through an inch of water on her tile floor.

"Old pipes, I'd say. Just about everything down here needs to be replaced."

"Great." She should have known this was not going to be one of her better days. "I don't suppose you have the number of a good plumber, do you?"

Lee came out from underneath the sink and stood up. "How about me?"

"You plumb, too?"

"I'm good on some things. This is one of them, so you're in luck. It's just a matter of taking out the old and putting in the new."

That helped her mood. So did the sight of his calm, confident smile. "Great," she repeated, this time without sarcasm.

"But we'll have to make a trip to a hardware store to get the pipes, some plumber's putty and maybe a wrench, if you don't have one."

"I do. It's a little rusty but it works. Would it save time if you wrote down what you need and I leave you here to start taking things apart, while I hit the hardware store?"

"It would, but—"

"I know. You're supposed to be my bodyguard and never let me out of your sight. But I think I can make it to the shopping center and back all right. It's only about six blocks away, broad daylight, and there'll be people everywhere."

"You're sure you want to do that?"

"Nobody is going to follow me, and just to make sure I'll pay special attention to the cars behind me. If I see anything suspicious I'll turn around and come back here with my horn blaring, so you'll know to run out and rescue me. I'll be fine." She glanced at the faucet. "Any chance that you could replace the whole tap, too? It's ancient, and the more I scrub off the finish, the more I think I need a new one, and I hate having to call someone to do those things."

"No problem. I'll have everything torn up, anyway."

"Then I'll get one of those, too." She headed for her mop in the laundry room. "Why don't you make a list while I clean up the water and find the wrench? Then we'd better both get out of these wet shoes.''

Lee couldn't have provided himself with a better stroke of luck. The minute Blythe left for the hardware store he headed for her bedroom.

In the doorway of the pale cream-colored room he paused. Going through the rest of her house had been an invasion, but even the bathroom hadn't seemed as off-limits as this did. The feminine ambience of the four-poster bed with its crocheted spread and lace pillow shams made him feel as if he was violating a sanctuary that held secrets, a place a man should only be *invited* to step into.

Then he remembered that she hadn't been concerned about Howard intercepting her outside the house and realized that must mean she'd left the formula behind. It was all the impetus he needed to step across the threshold and move toward the hope chest. Wasn't the formula her hope for the good life, after all?

Opening the lid, the first things he encountered were satin sheets. Black satin sheets.

He swallowed, mentally called himself a jerk, then trailed his fingertips across them, anyway. Cool and slippery and sensual....

Lee clenched his teeth and forced himself to set them aside before the image of Blythe's pale, naked skin against them grew any more vivid.

Below the sheets he found photograph albums full of what were apparently family pictures; old yearbooks; scrapbooks with ribbons from her grade school. Mementos emerged: crushed corsages, postcards, yellowed napkins and matchbooks from restaurants. Beneath that layer were more scrapbooks, these full of newspaper clippings he didn't bother to read.

But there was no formula, and once he was sure of that he quickly put everything back and closed the lid on it all.

Getting resolutely to his feet he went to the armoire. Opening its doors, Blythe's unmistakable scent wafted out and what he had avoided thinking too much about a moment before assaulted him, taking on a life of its own. He held his breath and willed the image of her to go away. He didn't want to see her warm and inviting and wanting him.

He shook his head as if that would clear it.

Think of Howard. Think of what she did to him.

That helped. Steeled with the aid of the new, if forced, mental picture of Blythe rummaging through his uncle's work and walking away with it, he managed to sort through the clothes hanging in the armoire, through the shoes that lay below.

He found nothing.

Then he opened the armoire's drawer. It held underwear. Lace-edged and silky.

Lee's palms grew sweaty.

He ran his open hands down his jean-clad thighs.

This was crazy, he told himself. He wasn't a pubescent boy, for God's sake.

Irritated, he reached into the drawer and fought images of Blythe wearing these bits of cloth as he searched for the papers she'd stolen from his uncle.

But EASY wasn't there, either.

"Where the hell is it?" he groused out loud.

He got down on his knees to look under the bed, then lay flat on his back to check the underside of the box springs. While still down there he felt beneath the top of her night table, then stood up and ran his hands under the mattress and checked the back of the headboard. Again he found nothing.

All that was left was a framed photograph on the wall, a picture of a Victorian porch with a wicker chair. Lee took it down and pulled away just enough of the brown paper backing to look behind it; that wasn't EASY's hiding place, either.

"She's good, I'll give her that," he grumbled. He had to concede that the formula wasn't in her bedroom. And he didn't know where else it could be, since he'd searched every square inch of her house. The only thing he'd come up with was the certainty that she was being damn careful not to give anyone the opportunity to do to her what she had done to Howard.

He took one more look around the room to see if he'd missed anything. He hadn't. But he had left everything in enough disarray to let her know what had been going on. The armoire doors were open, so he closed them. The drawer was slightly ajar, so he pushed it shut. The picture on the wall was lopsided. He straightened it, stepped back to make sure and straightened it a little more. Then he caught sight of a slip of paper on the floor near the hope chest.

He picked it up. It was a small newspaper clipping announcing the antibiotic discovery Blythe had told him about the night before. The one made by the first person she'd worked with.

Lee opened the hope chest and moved its contents until he reached the scrapbook that held other newspaper items. As he replaced the one he'd retrieved from the floor he remembered the conversation they'd had about her early work history. It would have been easy for her to have taken some of the credit for the other scientist's discovery, he reflected, especially when relating it to someone who wouldn't know the difference. But she hadn't done that. Instead, even when Lee had suggested that her contribution was greater than she'd said, she had denied it and insisted on giving credit where credit was due.

That wasn't what he'd expected from someone unethical enough to do what she had.

On the other hand, it was completely in keeping with what she seemed to be as a person.

Regardless of what she seemed to be, however, there was no denying that she had pirated Howard's formula, he reminded himself yet again. Or that she'd been involved in something similar five years ago. She just wasn't what she seemed.

Lee bent over her bed to straighten it. As he did so he started to wonder if those satin sheets in her hope chest were for future use or if she slept on them every night.

"This is getting kinky," he muttered.

But he couldn't help lifting the crocheted spread, pulling the edge of the blanket free and reaching underneath.

Satin.

Lee groaned. Why was he torturing himself? If one lousy, little aborted kiss had left him uncomfortable all last night, what was it going to do to him tonight to know that she was a few yards away, sleeping on those sheets?

He tucked her blanket back in and finished straightening the spread, wondering if the constant flip-flopping of his feelings between hot and cold would kill him before this was all over and done with.

"I'm sorry it took so long," Blythe said as she kicked the front door closed behind her an hour later.

Lee was on the floor with his head under the sink. He ducked out but stayed sitting there. "I was beginning to think you lost your way home."

"I just wanted to make certain I got it all," she said as she set the bag on the counter. "Everything okay?"

He shrugged. "Shouldn't it be?"

She could hardly say he had the cutest little worry line between his eyes, so she merely said, "Sure."

In one hand he held the wrench and in the other a rusty pipe. Tossing the pipe into the trash, he got to his bare feet with the lithe grace of a Russian dancer.

"Nobody called or... anything?" she asked.

"What did you do? Leave your formula here with me and then worry about it while you were gone?"

She had to smile at his attempt to ferret out the whereabouts of EASY, enjoying the realization that not knowing was driving him crazy. "Maybe I was just worried about you. Maude and Hershel could have gotten out and scared you to death."

"Not a chance—the first thing I did was shut the laundry room door."

She feigned a frown. "Poor babies, locked away like criminals."

"You know," he said as he took hardware out of the sack, one piece at a time, judged it and set it on the counter, "what makes me a little more nervous than your rats is not knowing where this formula of yours is."

This time she grinned. "No? Not really?" she said with exaggerated disbelief.

He ignored her teasing. "What if whoever ransacked this place was to barge in and start tearing through it again? You've tied my hands on bodily throwing him out. I think I should at least know where the formula is, so I could grab it and run with it. As things stand I wouldn't even know if the guy was close to finding it, let alone being able to get it out of harm's way."

All good points, Blythe conceded. But none of them mattered to her. Without malice she observed, "I understand, but I'd just feel a lot more comfortable being the only one to know where it is."

"Then it was here? You didn't take it with you?"

"It's safe," was all she would say before changing the subject. "I bought doughnuts, too."

"Let me guess—chocolate ones," he said, teasing her back.

She had to like this guy, she just couldn't help it, especially when he accepted defeat so graciously. "Of course. I take it you've noticed my predilection?"

He shot a glance at the jar of chocolate chips that was always at the ready on the counter. "Hard to miss it. Every time I get into the refrigerator for something to eat or into a cupboard, looking for a glass or a cup or a plate, I find more."

Blythe opened the box of doughnuts. "I could live on the stuff."

"Apparently." He chose an éclair and as he ate it, took the instructions out of the package that held the tap apparatus. When he'd read them through he surveyed everything on the counter and said, "Looks like we're all set. Want to play plumber's helper?"

"I couldn't very well leave you out here alone to do my household repairs, could I?"

His smile was quick and pleased. "No, you couldn't."

"Will it take all day?"

"And into the evening, since it's almost two o'clock and we're just starting."

"Is it that late? Guess I should have brought home hamburgers instead of doughnuts."

"It's okay, I'm not very hungry." He finished the last of the éclair, took several pipes and silver rings and sat down on the floor again.

"What do you need me for?" Blythe asked.

His grin was lascivious. "Loaded question." Then he leaned back under the sink. "Just be ready to hand me what I ask for."

Blythe brought a stepping stool close beside him and sat down on it, wrapping her arms around her knees. It was nice to have someone around who could do things like this. Ordinarily she'd have just been left in a mess until she could get a plumber to come and then she'd have had to worry about taking out a second mortgage to pay for it. Instead, everything was being taken care of right now and not only didn't she have to pay for it, she was being treated to a pretty nice view in the process.

Lee had on a white polo shirt that fitted like a glove around his chest and was tucked into the waistband of snug jeans that outlined muscular thighs. Her attention was caught by his feet—one of them flat on the floor to brace his bent knee and the other stretched out. Long and wide, they looked sturdy. His toes were boxy and big-knuckled like his hands, and the underside of the one she could see was a healthy rose color, clean and uncallused. She imagined it would feel like kidskin—tough and smooth and soft all at once. In her mind she felt it rub up and down her calf, those carelessly manicured toes of his curling around her shin.

A little flutter went off in her stomach.

Over his feet?

Very strange. She'd always had a particular distaste for feet. Anybody's feet. Yet there wasn't a single thing about Lee's that she found anything but...sexy.

Blythe realized her mouth was very dry.

"I have club soda in the fridge," she said, loudly enough for him to hear her. "Would you like some?"

"Maybe later, thanks."

She poured herself a large glassful and squeezed fresh lime into it.

"So what else do you eat besides chocolate, Stroganoff and pizza?" he asked as he emerged from the cupboard to throw another pipe away.

"Raspberries, coconut and peanut butter." She sat down on the stool again but steadfastly avoided looking at his feet this time.

"Ever heard of things called vegetables?"

"Ugly green things?"

"And some in white and yellow, too."

"Sounds gruesome."

He shook his head at her just before ducking back out of sight. "What do you like to do when you aren't working?"

"See friends, read, watch TV, go to the movies or museums, travel occasionally with my folks, play godmother to a couple of my friends' kids...." Her train of thought suddenly shifted when her gaze got as far as his ankles, thick and hairy.

"Wouldn't you like to have some of your own?"

Ankles? No, that wasn't what he was talking about. He meant kids. "I don't know, I used to think so, but lately I wonder if I'm too old."

Out he came again, giving her the once-over with those aquamarine eyes of his. "You're not. And you look in pretty good shape to me. In spite of a diet too heavy in the chocolate category."

She watched him rummage through the plumbing fittings until he found what he was looking for. "What about you? Do you want kids?" Blythe asked.

"A few. Someday soon, before I'm too old to hear them cry without turning up the volume on my hearing aid."

Blythe returned his once-over. "You might have a little time yet," she teased.

"A year or two, anyway," he answered wryly. "Hand me that wall flange—the doughnutlike thing that isn't a slip nut."

"Whatever a slip nut is." But she found what he'd described and passed it to him. "Where did you learn to be a plumber?"

"A do-it-yourself book. I also need the L-shaped pipe."

He lay back inside the cupboard then, giving instructions from there.

The afternoon evolved into the evening with more small talk and teasing. Blythe's job as assistant didn't require much, and as the hours passed she had a harder and harder time keeping her eyes off Lee. There was the way his muscles bulged from his shoulders and tapered to his waist. There was the flatness of his belly below the waistband of his pants. There were his thighs, hard and corded, stretching the denim of his jeans to the limit when they flexed. And there was the zipper to those jeans, dipping in here, bulging out there....

Blythe drank a lot of club soda.

They had Chinese food delivered around seven, and by the time they had finished eating and were back at work, she swore she was going to make her eyes behave themselves. And her mind along with them, while she was at it. Then Lee started to put the tap together, going up and down to work on the pipes below the sink and the faucet and handles above. And every time he stood, his rear end landed directly in front of her until Blythe just couldn't sit still anymore.

"If you don't need me I'll feed Maude and Hershel," she said, bolting from her stool.

Lee glanced over his shoulder. "Getting antsy?"

"No, I just forgot all about their dinner."

"Go ahead. I'm almost finished here, anyway, and I'll need you to turn on the water again."

Blythe snatched a bowl full of delectables for the mice and went into the laundry room.

A few minutes later Lee called, "Okay, I'm all set out here. Turn her on."

Too late. He'd already turned her on. Blythe swallowed and opened the water main.

"Dammit! Shut it off!"

She did and went into the kitchen, to find Lee backing out of the cupboard. He stood up and turned drenched hair, dripping face, and nearly transparent, clinging white shirt her way.

"I forgot to go back and tighten a joint," he explained as he wiped the tip of his nose with the back of his hand.

"I'll get you a towel," was all Blythe could say by way of an answer, making a fast retreat.

When she came back Lee was shirtless. Gloriously shirtless.

She handed him the towel and dived for the refrigerator and the club soda again. With some effort she managed not to look back at him as he tightened whatever it was he needed to tighten under the sink and told her she could try turning on the water main again.

"Perfect!" she heard him exclaim this time and could only agree, even though what she was thinking about was the way he looked without his shirt.

Since she could hardly hide in the laundry room forever, Blythe jammed her hands into her jeans pockets and stormed the kitchen with her sights set on the sink.

"It looks great," she managed. "Maybe you should hire out as The Bodyguard Plumber and double your rate." She tried the hot water and then the cold, swung the tap from right to left, squirted the spray nozzle.

"I only do this for special cases," he informed her.

It was a relief to know he didn't realize what she was struggling with. Enough of a relief for her to look at him again—if only in the eye. "I'll clean this up while you dry off."

"Actually I was thinking more of taking a shower. Plumbing is grimy work." He held out one metal-blackened hand to prove it.

"Go ahead," Blythe agreed, glad of a few minutes to get herself together.

Lee headed for the bathroom and Blythe went to work like a dervish on the mess of rust and water, old and new pipes and fittings, packaging and the debris of the day.

What was wrong with her? she wondered. Ogling the man like he was a picture on a beefcake calendar. Maybe it had been a long time since Jerry Nickles, and maybe there hadn't been anyone else in the interim, but that was no excuse for not being able to control herself.

When the mess was cleaned she went into the laundry room for a mop and bucket. Tomorrow she'd lock herself in there again and get a more reasonable perspective on Lee, she assured herself.

She went back to the kitchen and mopped the floor with a vengeance, feeling better with each swish of the mop.

When she finished, she dumped the dirty water into the washtub, rinsed the mop and hung it on a hook. Then she headed for the living room, intending to make up the couch to repay Lee for his plumbing efforts.

That was when she heard her name being called.

The first time she thought it was Lee needing something in the bathroom. The second time she realized it wasn't coming from inside the house.

It was Howard's voice.

Blythe grew very still while her heart doubled its pace. Her first instinct was to hide, but all the lights were on and she hadn't drawn the shade over the picture window. Through the thin, tiered curtains Howard would be able to see her move; he probably already knew she was there.

Blythe ran for the bathroom. "Lee? Lee, there's a problem."

"Another leak?" he asked through the door.

"No. The plumbing is fine, but now I could use the bodyguard half of your talents."

The bathroom door flew open and there he was, still shirtless, wearing a clean pair of jeans, zipped but not buttoned, his hair wet but combed. This time none of it had any effect on her.

"What's the matter?" he asked, looking down at her from beneath eyebrows that nearly met over the bridge of his nose.

She nodded toward the living room, just as Howard shouted for her from the front lawn. "He's who I need you to keep away," she said, a little feebly, she had to admit.

"Lock the door after me," he ordered, rushing past her.

Blythe followed, cringing at the sound of Howard's voice demanding that she let him in, that she give back his formula.

"Don't be rough," she called to Lee's back as he closed the door behind himself. She secured all three new locks and went to her room to look through the window, camouflaged by the darkness.

Lee met Howard halfway between her house and the curb, where a car was parked. She watched as Lee slid his hands into his back pockets. He looked calm, patient, in control of the situation, and Blythe had a sudden flash of pure gratitude; it was good to have him here.

Although Howard no longer shouted loudly enough for her to hear him, she could tell his voice was still raised and see him flail his arms about.

The sight of her former colleague so upset, so out of control made her stomach clench into a knot. "Just go home, Howard," she whispered. "Please, just go home."

Although the scene lasted only about ten minutes, it seemed like a year to Blythe. Finally, Lee walked the older man to the car at the curb. One last time Howard said something he accentuated with a jabbing index finger before getting into the vehicle. Lee stayed at the curb, looking down the street long after Howard had pulled away.

Blythe dropped her forehead to the cool glass of her window and took a few deep breaths, thanking God that the incident hadn't degenerated into something worse. Then she went back into the living room to let Lee in.

"It seemed as if you handled that just right," she told him as she relocked the door after him.

He looked as disturbed as she felt. "You were watching?"

Blythe collapsed onto the couch, dropping her head to its back. "I couldn't hear anything but I saw it all, yes." She sighed, certain of the cause of Lee's concerned expression as he silently questioned her from where he stood on the other side of the coffee table. "You got an earful, didn't you?"

"Yes, I did."

She knew he was waiting for an explanation, that he deserved one. Now he must be wondering if he was aiding and abetting her in doing something unethical, if not illegal. She just didn't know if she could confide in him.

"Do you want to tell me what's going on here?" he asked.

"It's complicated," she hedged. "And it isn't what it seems."

"It isn't?"

"No, it isn't. Could you just trust me on this?"

Lee finally rounded the coffee table and sat down next to her. He turned toward her, laying his arm along the sofa back. But he didn't say anything and she took his lack of pressure as concession.

"I appreciate that you didn't treat Howard roughly or with anything but respect," she said. "That was important to me."

"It seems pretty generous in view of some of the things he said." There was no baiting or accusation in his tone of voice; instead he sounded genuinely perplexed.

"What he said doesn't matter." Blythe sat up, hugging herself against the chill that had settled into her bones. In her mind's eye she saw Howard again as he'd been on the front lawn and something else occurred to her. "Do you think he was okay to drive home?"

"He wasn't drunk, if that's what you're thinking."

"No, I could tell he was just upset. But it worries me that maybe he was too agitated to operate a car."

"I didn't see any reason for him not to." Lee paused a moment. Then, apparently a little reluctantly, he added, "I don't understand your worrying about him."

She shrugged. "We've known each other since I was in graduate school. He was the professor and the head of CU's research department—the man I told you about the other night. We go way back." She tried to swallow the catch in her throat.

"This was the man who took you into his independent research group when your life fell apart?"

She nodded, managing only to say, "Yes."

"But now you're at odds."

"Unfortunately."

There was silence for a moment. "I think you mean that," he said, almost more to himself than to her, she realized.

"I do. Howard has been father, friend, mentor, savior.... Well, let's just say he's been a big part of my life."

"Then maybe you should try to patch things up, talk to him."

She shook her head. "That isn't possible."

"Anything is possible."

"Not that," she said sadly. Suddenly the thought of what she'd lost in Howard made her eyes fill with tears. She looked at Lee over her shoulder and tried to smile, to chase the unshed tears away. "I'm just glad you were here and nothing worse happened."

His pale eyes locked with hers and she had the sense that he was weighing something, hesitating. Then he reached a hand to the nape of her neck, squeezing gently, smoothing circles there with his thumb.

Reflexively she tilted her head slightly to free the way for his strong fingers, and somehow the next thing she knew her cheek was pressed against his bare chest. Warm and hard and smelling of soap, his body offered a comfort she needed at that moment.

Slowly she tipped her face up to him, only meaning to thank him. But he looked down at her with those gorgeous eyes and the words were forgotten. His face came nearer and stopped, as if he were giving her time to back up, the way she had last night.

She didn't.

He wrapped his arms around her and her body melded with his as if it were meant to be there. Nothing in her made her want to be anywhere else.

Then he leaned forward, pressing his lips against hers very lightly at first. So lightly that Blythe deepened the kiss herself; tentativeness was not what she craved. She closed her eyes and lost herself to the tenderness of his mouth.

She laid her palms on his chest and answered the parting of his lips with the parting of her own. No longer tentative at all, Lee deepened the kiss and made it everything she had imagined it would be all through the past night and off and on all day long as she'd watched him work. Sensual and warm and wonderful.

Then common sense reared its ugly head.

She was vulnerable, she knew, after Howard's appearance. And after so little sleep and so many hours of less than pure thoughts about Lee, it was easy to be carried away. But starting anything personal with this man was an additional complication in an already complicated situation. Right now she just didn't think she could handle anymore.

Blythe ended the kiss, using that hard chest to push herself away. "Maybe this isn't such a good idea."

Lee's arms dropped from around her but one finger came back to trace the curve of her cheekbone with a gentle knuckle. "Maybe you're right," he agreed, the raspiness of his voice telling of the impact of that kiss on him, too.

"Crazy night," she commented with a small laugh.

"Full moon," he added.

"And the werewolves are out." She took a breath, slapped both of her hands down on her knees and stood up. "I think I'd better go to bed."

"Want me to check under it for bogeymen before you do?" he teased quietly.

The image of Lee in her bedroom for any reason at all sent a skitter up her spine. She tried to ignore it and forced a smile. "Thanks, but the dust bunnies under there keep it bogeyman free." She fought the strongest urge to stay with him, to taste more of that kiss, to just plain taste more of him. But she couldn't, she told herself. She didn't dare. "Good night," she managed with some difficulty.

"Good night," he answered.

Blythe escaped before her will grew any weaker.

Chapter Five

As she made her bed the next morning Blythe wondered if her life was in some sort of cycle—every five years it went haywire.

What other explanation could there be for fate sending Lee now, of all times, when the last thing she needed was the eruption of the feelings he was causing in her? A simple, single kiss, and adrenaline had kept her awake half the night, leaving her feeling the same way she had after her first kiss twenty years ago.

The phone rang just as she was finishing that side of the bed and she picked up the receiver before the machine could ring again.

"Did I wake you?" her brother asked after she'd said hello.

"No, I was up."

"I just wanted to know how things are going."

"Funny you should ask," Blythe said, sitting down on the bed as she told him about the night before.

"Thank goodness you weren't alone. I didn't think Howard would give up," Gib commented when she'd finished. "Are you any closer to breaking the formula?"

"The last couple of days haven't exactly been conducive to work. And besides everything else, Lee is sort of a distraction."

"Speaking of which, the guy I talked to at the Executive Protection Agency called yesterday. He didn't leave much of a message on my machine, just that he'd call back. I imagine he's checking up, probably wants to know if we're satisfied."

As bodyguards went, Blythe couldn't be more satisfied with Lee. On the other hand, as her body went, she was a long way from being satisfied. Frustrated, yes, but not satisfied. Not that it was something she wanted to tell her brother. "Well, after last night I can honestly say he's doing a great job. He handled the situation with Howard perfectly."

"And you were worried he'd be all brawn and no brains," Gib reminded her smugly.

"You don't have to rub it in. I admit I was wrong. There were no strong-arm tactics last night. He used calm diplomacy to get Howard to go home."

"Quite a guy, huh?"

Oh, yes. "I also owe him one for not coming in afterward with accusations and condemnations. I know Howard had to have told him all about my taking his formula."

"And Lee didn't say anything?"

"He was curious, but when I said I didn't want to talk about it, he dropped it." And instead treated her kindly,

compassionately. Someone else might have demanded
that she at least confirm or deny Howard's claims.
Someone else might have left her high and dry rather than
chance being involved in something of questionable ori-
gin. Someone else surely would have had a change in attitude toward her. But not Lee. "He was actually great
about it. I really felt as if he was on my side in spite of
what he'd heard."

"Do I hear admiration in your voice?"

"Appreciation," she corrected. Still, she couldn't deny
that she was getting a soft spot for the guy. He had brains
to go with his not overly developed brawn. He had charm
and sensitivity, a sense of humor, and no-doubt-about-it-
sensuality that he didn't even seem to realize he possessed. He wasn't arrogant or vain or cocky, the way
someone else who looked like he did might be.

"Anyway," she went on, "this bodyguard idea of
yours was a good one. I don't know what I'd have done
without him last night."

"Now I'm hearing affection."

"Gratitude."

"But having his constant company isn't proving to be
a hardship?" Gib goaded her.

Blythe found herself rolling her eyes. "No, it isn't a
hardship."

"You'd say it's bearable, then?"

"Bearable."

"Enjoyable?"

"Passably."

"Pleasant?"

Blythe sighed into the phone. "He's a nice, personable, charming, easy-to-get-along-with guy. Okay?"

"And aren't you touchy about it! When we were kids and I teased you about boys, you only got that way when you had a crush on one."

"Don't you think my life is complicated enough at the moment without starting something up with my body-guard?"

"I don't know. What do you think?"

"I don't have to think about it. Things are definitely too messed up right now to have hot thoughts about Lee."

"Hot thoughts, huh?"

Gib sounded so much like he had when they were kids that she had to laugh in spite of herself. "Yes, hot thoughts," she conceded.

"Do you need a chaperon over there?"

"What I need is to take a shower so I can go to work for the day."

"A cold one?"

"I'll talk to you later."

Blythe hung up. She put on her robe, hid her under-wear between the clean clothes she would wear for the day and slipped quietly from her room to the bathroom, so as not to wake Lee.

Once behind the locked door she turned on the water in the shower and opened the linen closet to get her soap and sponge. But they were blocked by the leather Dopp Kit, and as had been the case since Lee had put it there, it drew her attention. This time it was open.

Looking into it was a very strange thing to want to do, she told herself as she reached over the brown bag for her shower gear.

She wanted to, just the same.

It would be an invasion of his privacy and it wasn't any of her business, she told herself. But rather than turning back to her shower she stood there, facing the Dopp Kit.

He hadn't bothered to close it, she reasoned. And it was right there under her nose, with her own things next to it, all in plain sight. He looked at them every day.

She craned her neck just a little.

So he used a straight razor instead of an electric one. Funny how vivid the image was that popped into her mind of his face lathered, his chest bare as he shaved.

Blythe leaned a little nearer and caught a whiff of his after-shave in the bottle beside the razor. Heady stuff. She took another draft of the scent, savoring both it and the little skitter of goose bumps that erupted on her skin.

With one index finger she pushed the razor and after-shave aside. There was toothbrush and paste. Mouthwash. Floss.

The memory of his mouth against hers was ripe, and only after a moment did she realize that her lips had grown slack at the thought.

She swallowed and told herself to get into the shower.

Instead she nudged those articles out of the way and kept on snooping.

Deodorant. Comb and brush. Shampoo in a small bottle from a hotel in Seattle.

Howard's nephew Bucky was working there.

The thought of Howard helped bring her back to earth.

She straightened and moved away from the shelf.

What was she doing, anyway? Getting light-headed over a man's travel kit? Getting hot and bothered over his toothpaste, of all things? So what if he was a man who took care of himself without being flashy about it?

She was a grown woman. A scientist. One whiff of after-shave and a clandestine peek at deodorant should not be enough to let butterflies loose in her stomach.

Blythe closed the linen closet door as if she were trapping something inside. The bathroom was full of steam and she hadn't even set foot in the shower yet. How long had she been standing there?

She dropped her robe to the floor, flung off the T-shirt she wore for pajamas and stepped over the side of the tub into the warm spray.

Blythe was almost surprised that it didn't make a sizzling sound when it hit her skin.

Things were just a little crazy now. That was all there was to it.

The sound of the shower water woke Lee. He opened his eyes, then shut them again in a hurry against the sting left by a second night with almost no sleep.

Not that he hadn't tried. Unlike the one before when he'd searched for the formula, he'd spent the last night tossing and turning as the confrontation with his uncle replayed itself over and over in his mind.

"Bucky! What are you doing here?" Howard had greeted him on the front lawn.

"What do you mean, what am I doing here?" Lee had asked, wondering if his uncle had actually not realized he'd be staying with Blythe at night, too. "I told you that I'm playing bodyguard, and bodyguards stick around twenty-four hours a day. A better question is what are *you* doing here?"

Howard had been so stirred up, he'd ranted, "I'm not going to let her get away with this. That's what I'm doing here."

"No, that's why I'm here."

As the scene repeated itself in his head, Lee realized that it sounded like some kind of comedy routine for the Three Stooges. Only in this situation it wasn't funny.

Lee coaxed his eyes open more carefully.

Aggie was right, he thought. Howard was more upset over this whole business than he'd realized. All the while Lee had tried to convince his uncle to leave and not come back, to let him handle this situation, Howard had ranted about getting back what was his. It had been hard to tell if the older man had heard a word he'd said.

Now, with Blythe in the shower, there was no time like the present to find out.

Lee swung off the couch, pulled on his pants and went to the phone. It was his uncle who answered on the third ring.

"Bucky!" Howard greeted him, sounding like his old, familiar self. "Are you calling with good news?"

Lee hated bursting his uncle's bubble, especially after seeing him as riled as Howard had been the night before. "No, I'm afraid not. I just wanted to make sure you were all right," he said as he slipped out the back door the way he had the morning before.

"I'm just fine, considering that I don't have EASY and I could have had a better night's sleep."

"Instead of coming here to raise hell on the front lawn and nearly blowing my cover," Lee added.

Howard's laugh sounded slightly embarrassed. Lee's first inclination was to relieve that feeling in his uncle. But he knew he had to make his point. "I meant what I said last night."

"What did you say last night?" Howard asked with an uneasy chuckle, as if making a joke out of it would lessen his awkwardness.

"You have to stay away from here, Howard."

"From your house?"

"I'm serious. You know what I'm talking about. Don't come anywhere near Blythe Coopersmith's house again."

"She better hope I don't," his uncle grumbled.

"*I* hope you don't. She couldn't hear what either of us said on the lawn last night, so she still doesn't realize who I am, but your coming here was too close for comfort. If she figures out that we're related, she'll throw me out on my ear and we'll never get EASY back."

There was silence before Howard spoke again. "You feel confident that you can, then, is that it?"

"Reasonably. But only if you stay away."

"From her house."

Maybe his uncle had just woken up, too. "Yes, from her house. I'm with her every minute, so it's only a matter of time before I get my hands on the formula. The only thing that could go wrong is her finding out who I am, and that won't happen if you steer clear of here."

"Well, you know I'll do whatever I have to to get my formula back, Bucky," Howard said, reasonably enough, Lee thought.

"Good. Then just sit tight and let me handle it."

"You'll keep me posted?"

"I'll try, but it's tempting fate to make these calls. Besides, until I get my hands on your papers there isn't much to tell you. Just trust me."

"I always have."

"Until last night."

"Oh, don't pay me any attention," Howard said, the chagrin back in his voice. "Your aunt says I've gone off the deep end over this formula."

That sounded like Aggie. It made Lee smile and give in to the urge to ease his uncle's discomfort about what was obviously a rash act the night before, probably out of sleeplessness that had left him thinking too much about the wrong that had been done him. "I wouldn't go so far as to say you've gone off the deep end. Just try to relax and leave it to me. I won't let you down."

"I know you won't, Bucky."

Lee sneaked back into the house and hung up. He was glad he'd called. He hadn't realized how worried he was about his uncle until hearing Howard back to normal relieved his uneasiness. What was more of a surprise to him was the feeling that he should tell Blythe and ease her concerns from last night, too.

Very strange.

But if he was honest with himself he realized that he believed the care she'd shown for Howard was genuine, not just an act. After all, why would she pretend to worry whether or not his uncle was too upset to drive? It was clear that her insistence that no force be used was the result of a guilty conscience. That was probably why she was worrying about the well-being of the man she'd exploited, too.

But what about the underlying regret he'd heard in her allusions to what she'd done? Was it possible that she was really sorry for it? But if that was the case, why wouldn't she just return EASY? Sure, it would be embarrassing. But at least Howard would have his formula back.

Or was there something else?

Was it possible that Blythe had some overwhelming need for the money EASY would generate? Was there some other reason, someone or something that had *forced* her to appropriate EASY? Some reason that kept her from righting the wrong she'd done? That compelled her to go on with what she'd started, even though she regretted it?

As he thought about it, Lee gathered clean clothes for his own shower, since he no longer could hear the water running.

Someone or something forcing her to take the formula against her will seemed a little too melodramatic to buy into. Yet the idea of a driving need better fitted the person he was getting to know than the thought that she was a conniving double-crosser who hid her real nature with accomplished acting.

But what could that driving need be? And why wouldn't she have gone to Howard with her problems? After all, he'd bailed her out before.

Remembering that past incident shook the foundation of Lee's newfound explanation for what had made Blythe take Howard's formula in the first place. Had she had a justifiable reason then, too? Much as he wanted to believe it, it didn't seem likely.

Yet his gut instinct told him that theory was more plausible than the idea of Blythe being a conniving double-crosser.

Or was his gut instinct being influenced by the attraction for her?

He didn't know. He honestly couldn't tell.

He only knew that for every minute he spent with her, that attraction grew stronger. Strong enough for him to believe she'd felt compassion for Howard last night. Strong enough for Lee not to be able to resist the urge to comfort her. Strong enough for that urge to turn instantly into plain, simple desire for her as a woman.

But as long as there was any possibility that Blythe had a good reason for taking EASY, he couldn't condemn her. And while he was looking for the formula, he decided, he'd try to get to the bottom of all this.

* * *

The first thing Lee saw when he left the bathroom after his shower was Blythe feeding Maude and Hershel on the island counter. Why did she have to look so damn appealing? he thought. But there she was, radiating that fresh-scrubbed, girl-next-door quality, her thick, curly hair pulled low on her nape in a ponytail, wearing a plum-covered V-necked T-shirt and jeans that cupped her small rear end just the way his hand itched to.

"I hope I didn't use up all the hot water," she said, smiling at him in that way that made her eyes light up and glisten.

"I had plenty," he answered, tearing his gaze away.

"Have you been okay sleeping on the couch?" she asked.

She sounded like someone trying to make idle conversation to ease the tension of a first date. Lee didn't have a doubt that the kiss that had ended the evening before was on her mind. Hell, it was on his, too, even with all the other things he should be thinking of. He took the coffeepot to the sink and filled it. "The couch is comfortable enough," he answered. His discomfort was all internal. "What's on the agenda today?"

"I'm afraid I need to work," she said. "I hated missing yesterday."

"Why is that? Are you a workaholic, or is there some hurry?"

The soft, lilting sound of her laugh sprinted up his spine and erased the ground he'd gained by not looking at her. "I guess I have been a workaholic the past few years," she said. "Are you getting cabin fever from being cooped up? If you have something you'd like to do to get out for awhile, I'll be okay here by myself."

After seeing Howard the way he'd been the night before, Lee realized that he couldn't rest if he left Blythe alone. Add one more item to the list of oddities in this situation. "I thought I'd mow your grass," he said with a nod out the window over the sink.

Blythe groaned. "I know I should have had it done by now. Usually I call my lawn-mowing person to start in the middle of April, but this year things have just gotten away from me. Don't feel as if you have to do it. Plumbing was above and beyond the call of duty. You definitely don't have to play gardener now, too."

"I'd like the exercise." And for some reason he liked the idea of performing domestic services for her. Maybe the lack of sleep these past two nights was getting to him.

Lee took down the bag of bagels from the cupboard. As he did he caught sight of Blythe bent close to the cage, cooing to her mice as she crumbled more food into their dish. Her lips were puckered up, and deep in the pit of his stomach there was an answering tightening at the thought of having been the recipient of something similar last night. It didn't help to drag his gaze away, only to find that her rear end jutted out so near to his thigh that if he were to move the slightest little bit, he could bump into that small, firm bit of feminine flesh and she'd never know it was premeditated.

The doorbell rang just then and saved him from himself.

"Will you get that for me?" Blythe asked without looking away from what she was doing. "These babies are gluttons today."

"Gluttonous rats and she calls them babies," Lee goaded her as he headed for the door, glad of something to do that put distance between them. If he pulled the door open a little too forcefully, it was only a venting of pent-up frustration.

Still, it clearly startled the mailman standing outside. "I have a registered letter for—" the uniformed man glanced at the address "—for Blythe Coopersmith. No one else can sign for it," he said in an uneasy rush.

"Oh, okay. I'm coming," Blythe called before Lee had a chance to wade through what he was thinking.

He stepped aside when she came to the door, watching as she filled the mailman's requirements. When the letter had been duly delivered, Lee followed her back to the island counter in the kitchen, where she set down the unopened envelope and went back to feeding Maude and Hershel as if nothing had interrupted her.

"You're not going to open it?"

"No," she said, leaving it at that for a moment. Then she elaborated. "It's the proof of origination for the formula."

Just what he'd been afraid of. "You hadn't done it before?" he asked, surprised to find how much he'd been hoping he was wrong in assuming that was what the registered letter held.

"It's done now. That's all that matters," she said evasively.

Lee stared at the letter, wondering why the sight of it made it harder to believe she'd pirated the formula out of necessity. And yet, he reasoned with himself, if need had prompted her to take EASY in the first place, need would have demanded that she also cover her tracks so the formula could be attributed to her.

Somehow that didn't make him feel any better. He wanted to pick up that envelope and pocket it, wipe away its existence for Howard's sake—and for his own, too.

But of course he couldn't do that.

He pushed back his feelings and reminded himself that he had to keep a clear head. "You aren't going to leave it lying around, are you?"

"No." She laughed. "I'm just going to finish feeding the guys here and then I'll put it away."

"You have somewhere safe in mind, or do you need my help?"

"I'll just put it with the formula until I have time to take it to the bank and put it in a safety deposit box."

Which meant Lee had to get his hands on it before she did, because getting the formula back wouldn't do his uncle any good if she could open that envelope in court—which would have an earlier postmark than the one his uncle was just now compiling—and show a judge her own name as the creator of the idea. If he watched where she went with the letter, he thought, he'd at least know what room her hiding place was in, so he could tear it apart the next time he had the chance.

"Want a bagel for breakfast?" he offered.

"Sure," she said as she took the mouse cage to the laundry room.

When she came back she picked up the registered letter. Out of the corner of his eye Lee watched her as she rounded the island counter and headed down the hall. But before she'd gone two steps the doorbell rang again.

"Busy place this morning," she commented, setting the letter back on the counter and heading for the front of the house.

As Lee buttered their bagels he heard her open the door and a male voice ask if she was Blythe Coopersmith.

When she answered that she was the visitor said, "Is it true that you stole the formula for a weight-loss miracle discovered by Howard Horvat?"

Lee dropped what he was doing and went to the door. Blythe's face was white, her mouth slightly agape. But that didn't stop the man from shooting more questions at her.

"Are you aware that Howard Horvat is willing not to press charges against you if you will only return what you've taken? Can you tell me exactly what this miracle cure for fat is?"

"Uh . . . no. . . ."

It was obvious that Blythe was stunned and didn't know what to say to the skinny man's questions. Lee took her arm and moved her away from the door, saying, "No comment," as he closed it.

"Oh, my God," Blythe breathed when she went to the picture window. Lee joined her there, seeing another car stop at the curb across the street. On the side of the white station wagon was a large blue figure nine—the logo for a local television station.

Then the phone rang.

"Are you okay, Blythe?" he asked her as she looked from the front door that the skinny man was pounding to the ringing telephone.

"I just can't believe it," she said, plainly more to herself than to him.

Lee left her to answer the phone with a curt hello. The woman on the other end identified herself as a reporter from a local newspaper and asked for an exclusive interview that would give Blythe a chance to tell her side of the story.

"Where did you get this information?" Lee asked. He knew there could be only one source, but had to have it confirmed before he could believe it.

"Howard Horvat himself called a few minutes ago with the information," the woman on the other end said.

"Ms. Coopersmith isn't giving interviews," Lee informed her, hanging up without waiting to hear what the woman was proposing.

No sooner had the receiver hit the cradle than the phone rang again. This time Lee ignored it, turning to Blythe, who was straining to look over the tiered curtains from a distance, now that there were people drawing nearer to the house and the window itself.

"There's more of them coming," she said.

Lee could see the cars and news vans outside that lined both curbs of the street out front; the people were gathering on the lawn. The phone and the doorbell kept ringing, and from the yard a man shouted for Blythe to come out and talk to them, to defend herself if these allegations weren't true.

Why would Howard do this?

But with the front yard turning into a three-ring circus Lee didn't have time to think about it. "We have to get out of here," he told her as Blythe charged to the picture window and pulled the shade against the increasing shouts coming from the lawn.

"I'm in your hands," she said a little feebly when she turned back to him, her face ashen.

"I know a house we can use. Go pack just what you can take in one small bag."

"How are we going to get out of here?"

"They have your car blocked in the driveway, but we can get mine away from the curb. We'll just have to wade through them."

She nodded, looking so disoriented that it clenched his gut and made it hard for him to remember she wasn't the victim in this. "Make that phone stop ringing, will you?" she asked.

He picked it up without putting it to his ear, pressed the plunger just long enough to sever the connection, then laid the receiver on the counter.

"Thank you," she said and sighed as she headed down the hall.

When Lee saw her disappear into her bedroom he went to the phone. Once he'd dialed his uncle's number he stretched the cord into the laundry room and closed the door.

Howard answered, sounding different from the way he had two hours before—abrupt, agitated.

Lee didn't beat around the bush. "I'm in the middle of a three-ring circus of reporters and news hounds. Why did you alert the media?"

Lee half expected his uncle to deny it. Or maybe he wanted him to deny it so he could find that someone else had done this. But instead Howard answered with the same intensity he'd had the night before. "I called every newspaper and radio and television station in the phone book so I could shame her into giving my formula back, Bucky."

"That doesn't make any sense," Lee told him, trying to hold on to his patience. "What about keeping this quiet because you didn't want to bring nuts out of the woodwork who might try taking the formula away from her? Why didn't we just call the police in the beginning, if you wanted public exposure?"

"In the beginning?" Howard shouted. "This *is* just the beginning! I'm going to get national news interested next—"

"Howard—"

"I'm going to expose her for what she is—"

"Howard—"

"I'm going to make it so she can't show her face outside until she gives EASY back! I'm going to make her
rue the day she even thought about swiping my formula—"

"Howard!" Lee finally raised his own voice and his
uncle stopped. It was clear there was no reasoning with
him, so Lee said, "Let me talk to Aggie."

"Fine. Talk to her. I have a girl here from the *Rocky
Mountain News* that needs my story, anyway."

"Howard, don't—" But Lee's words didn't keep his
uncle on the line. Instead his aunt came on.

"What's going on there?" Lee asked.

"He's a man possessed this morning," Aggie said for-
lornly. "Just after he talked to you a little while ago, he
started stewing about what that woman's done to him.
Then he said he had a brainstorm and he got out the
phone book and started telling anybody he could get to
talk to him."

"Well, I'm in one hell of a mess here because of it,"
Lee said, realizing only after he'd barked the words out
that his aunt didn't deserve it. He amended his tone.
"I'm going to have to take Blythe and the formula away.
Can you keep Howard in check somehow before he does
anything to make this worse?"

"I've already persuaded him to go to the cabin. He's
been so upset, I thought it might do him some good to get
out of the city."

Where Howard would be too far from Denver to make
any impromptu visits and where there wasn't even a telephone. That, at least, was good news. "Can you get him
out before he says any more to the reporter there now?"

"No, I can't. He had two stipulations when he finally
agreed—that we wouldn't leave until after the interview
and that we'd come home first thing Monday morning.

He's so agitated, he can hardly sit still.'' Aggie's voice quivered slightly. But then Lee heard her sigh and when she went on there was nothing but anger in her tone. ''I could wring that woman's neck for doing this to him. I've never seen him the way he is over it. EASY was the most important thing he'd ever done and to have it slipped out from under his nose has just set him off. If you don't get that formula back, Lee, I don't know what will happen to your uncle.''

Lee pinched the bridge of his nose. ''I'll get it back, don't worry. Just take Howard away, so I can concentrate on it without him throwing me any more curves.'' He said goodbye to his aunt, left the laundry room and hung up the phone.

He hadn't thought this mess could get any worse, but he'd been wrong. And it wasn't made any easier by the inexplicable fact that he felt very protective toward Blythe. Of all the ways this situation could have been handled, he didn't agree with making it a public spectacle. Not for anyone's sake.

A resurgence of the doorbell and the phone both ringing at once brought him out of his reflection. He'd forgotten to leave the phone off the hook. Doing as he had before, he disconnected the call. Then he dialed again.

There was no time to think about anything but getting Blythe and EASY out of here.

He was going to need some help.

Chapter Six

"Are you a thief, Ms. Coopersmith?"

"Is it true that you've taken a formula which you didn't even contribute to?"

"We understand you were involved in an identical situation five years ago—would you care to comment on that?"

"Wouldn't you like to refute what's been said about you?"

"If what Mr. Horvat claims isn't true, why won't you talk about it? Why are you running away?"

The reporters clustered around like bees to a hive and moved en masse as Blythe and Lee made their way out of the front door. For the first time Blythe was sorry that her house sat so far back from the street.

She hugged Maude and Hershel's cage to her stomach and kept her eyes down because every time she looked up, camera lights flashed, almost blinding her. Lee poked a path through the cluster of pushing, prodding people with the two small suitcases he carried in his left hand. His right arm was around Blythe's shoulders, holding her tightly to his side; more than his imposing determination, the shelter of that big body of his was what got her through. Gib had never had a better idea than hiring Lee.

At a snail's crawl while one question more prying and goading than the next was fired at her, they finally made it to the curb and Lee's car. He took his arm from around her and reached for the door handle, but before he could get it open, a young blond woman with the body of a house wrecker lunged into his way.

"Is it true that you have in your possession a miracle cure for weight reduction that will change the way the whole world diets?" she demanded, thrusting a microphone into Blythe's face.

"Move," Lee ordered in a voice that was at once quiet and threatening.

"Just answer that one question, Ms. Coopersmith," the reporter said in a tone that matched Lee's.

Blythe raised her head and met the woman's challenging stare in spite of the bright white light that glared from a television camera on the other side of Lee's car. "I'm not going to answer any questions," she said, glad her voice came out as strongly as she'd intended.

"Now get the hell out of the way or I'll move you myself," Lee added.

"Do you mean for us to take your silence as an admission of guilt?" the woman taunted her.

Lee didn't say anything else. He just took a step forward and the reporter moved aside as if he were an oncoming truck.

A split second later Blythe was in Lee's car. She settled the mouse cage in her lap and tried to comfort poor

Maude and Hershel, who were cowering in a corner, as Lee went around to the driver's side and got in.

"You doing okay so far?" he asked as he started the engine.

"Sure," she said, trying to sound less disturbed than she felt.

Then she glanced out the side window. The whole crowd of people had dispersed, running like mad to the their cars, trucks and vans.

"Looks like we get to lead the parade," Lee observed as he pulled away from the curb and two cars behind him nearly collided in their hurry to follow.

"I hope you have a plan to lose them," Blythe said.

"All taken care of."

And strange as it was under the circumstances, that was how she felt. It suddenly struck her that Lee Farrell seemed like the best thing that had happened to her in a long time. "I don't know what I would have done without you," she said, glancing at his strong profile.

He smiled and looked at her out of the corner of his eye for just a moment. "You could have called the police and had them all removed as trespassers."

Blythe breathed a wry half laugh at that. "Then they would have sat across the street like vultures on a branch, just waiting for me to leave my property. Not to mention that I'd have had questions from the police to contend with then, too."

Lee merged into the highway traffic and Blythe looked out the side window. Mention of the police turned her thoughts to Howard and what his alerting the media meant.

If he had called the authorities it would have been difficult enough for her. But public humiliation was a whole different can of worms. A can she hadn't expected him to open.

The media wanted a scandal more than substantiation. And when everything was over, the resolution— even if it appeared in the press—wouldn't be what stuck in the minds of anyone who had heard about the accusations. What had happened with Jerry Nickles had never gotten media coverage. The damage that had wrought on her life and career had all been within her field. But this could be far worse.

For a moment she wanted to throw her hands up in the air, give back the damn formula and forget everything.

But she couldn't do that and she knew it. Taking EASY hadn't been a whim and she couldn't give it back on a whim, either. Besides, the can of worms was already open. Nothing could close it again now.

Lee eased off the highway and headed for downtown Denver, casting her a reassuring smile as he did.

What about him? Blythe asked herself. What must he think of all of this? Nothing good. But if that was the case, he hid it well. Or was it just part of his job to keep his own opinions and feelings to himself? A bodyguard didn't have to like the body he was guarding, after all; he just had to keep it out of harm's way.

Still, instinct told her he didn't think the worst of her. At the very least he was giving her the benefit of the doubt. That seemed more like him. And surely he couldn't have kissed her the way he had the past night if he believed what Howard had told him. Somehow that made her feel much better. It was almost as if his faith in her was enough to counteract whatever misfortune might come out of this new turn of events.

The office buildings of metropolitan Denver loomed above them on either side as Lee turned down Champa

Street. "This is where it gets a little dicey," he told her. "Hang on."

He hit his horn and the accelerator at once, turning on two wheels into the parking garage of one of the buildings. Before they were more than halfway through, the gate began to close, so that there was no time for any of the vehicles behind them to follow.

The squeal of Lee's tires echoed in the garage as he weaved his way down to a level below the street and into a parking place beside a bakery delivery van.

"Pastries, anyone?" he inquired as he lunged out of the car, dragging the suitcases with him.

Blythe didn't know what he had planned, but wasn't about to wait around for an explanation. Clutching the mouse cage in front of her, she was out of her side before he'd made it all the way around.

Then the door on the delivery van opened and a not-too-tall, chubby man with a receding hairline climbed down from the high seat.

"Blythe, my friend Chad Ingalls. Chad, meet Blythe Coopersmith, Maude and Hershel."

"Mice?" Chad asked, showing his distaste. "There's pies and cakes in the back of this van. It's bad enough I'm going to put you two in there with them. I can't let mice around that stuff."

"Can you leave the rats behind?" Lee asked Blythe in a hurry.

She shook her head. "I'm sorry, but I need them."

"They'll have to go up with you, Chad."

The shorter man took the cage and set it on the floor in front of the passenger seat. Then he went around to the rear of the van and opened the door there. "All aboard."

Within minutes Blythe and Lee were sitting on the floor between the wire racks that lined either side of the van, some of them laden with trays of sweets. Then they were immersed in darkness as Chad closed the rear door.

Seconds later the van bounced slightly, letting them know the portly man had gotten behind the wheel. As he started the engine, a panel that separated the cab from the back opened just a fraction of an inch. "Here we go," Chad said, then he closed the panel again and took away even that ribbon of light, leaving Blythe and Lee in the dark again.

"The exit for this garage is on the other side of the building, on a one-way street going the opposite direction from where we just came in. Our entourage can't get there without going across the Sixteenth Street Mall and around two blocks. We'll be long gone by the time they do, and even if somebody makes it, all they'll see is this delivery truck. Hopefully no one will think to follow it," Lee explained.

Sitting on the floor of the van, Blythe fought to keep from falling over every time they turned a corner. But a particularly sharp one caused her to bang her shoulder against Lee. He reached out and steadied her. Then, with a hand on each of her shoulders, he repositioned her so that she was braced against his side, his arm behind her, resting on one of the bakery racks.

They rode silently and Blythe became more and more aware of Lee, of his size and strength and hardness against her. The strangest part of it was that it felt so right, as if she fitted, belonged there, as if being there gave her more than physical balance. It also gave her emotional support that left her feeling that she could handle the mess she'd gotten herself into.

It occurred to her how many facets there were to what he made her feel. She enjoyed his company and his sense of humor in the same way she enjoyed her friends. She

OVER EASY127

felt as comfortable with him as she did with Gib, as safe as she had as a child in the protective circle of a parents' arms, as intellectually stimulated as she had with Howard. There was also the sensual side. Never in her life, not even with Jerry Nickles, had she been so easily or so powerfully turned on by the mere thought of a man, by just the sight of him, by the simplest of kisses or the barest brush of his hands.

"Where are we going?" she inquired when she realized she had trusted him so completely she hadn't even asked.

"Genesee Park." His voice sounded deeper echoing off the metal walls and she felt his chest rumble under her arm, much the way the van was vibrating beneath her.

"There's a house up there," he went on. "Chad's house. He's going to let us use it while he cohabits with the woman he's marrying next month."

Lee's friend opened the panel just then, flooding the rear of the van with light that momentarily blinded them. "Coast is clear, we're out of the city," Chad said. "Want to come up here?"

"I'll take the console if you want the seat," Blythe offered.

"Since I won't fit on the console, I'll take you up on it," he said.

It took a few wobbly attempts, but by the time Chad was on the highway headed toward the elite community in the foothills of the Rocky Mountains, Lee was in the passenger seat and Blythe was on the console with Maude and Hershel's cage in her lap once more.

The drive to Genesee only took about half an hour. When they got there Chad eased off the highway and onto a winding road until he was forced to stop at a gate where a uniformed man stepped out of a small brick hut.

One look into the van and he seemed to recognize both Lee and Chad. He waved and reached back into the guardhouse, apparently to operate the gate that opened within seconds.

From there the house wasn't far up the road. A split-level, it was part honey-colored brick and part natural wood in a modern style that still managed to mesh with the surrounding pine and fir trees, wildflowers and grasses. And there were enormous windows everywhere.

Lee leaned forward, looking around her, and said, "I was telling Blythe that you're loaning us your house while you live with Marcie until the wedding."

"Your bakery must be very successful," Blythe put in as they turned into the steep driveway that led to a garage on the lower level of the house.

Chad chuckled and threw a sidelong glance at Lee. "I'm doing better than I would as a bodyguard," he said, in what seemed to be a private joke between the two of them.

As Lee helped her down from the van, Chad took the suitcases from the back.

"The key is still on the top of the doorjamb, isn't it?" Lee inquired as they headed up the four stone steps to the front of the house.

"Unless someone I don't know moved it," Chad answered.

Lee found the key and opened the door, holding it for Blythe to go in first. She went through the mossy, rock-lined walls of the entranceway into a sunken living room. Decorated without any feminine touches, the navy-blue and cream-colored furniture had a masculine charm of its own. A loose-cushioned couch and matching chairs were arranged to face a wall of windows that framed a panoramic view of Denver. Bean-pot lamps stood on low end tables, a big-screen TV took up one whole corner and beside it stood an elaborate stereo system. A freestanding wood-burning fireplace that looked like an old potbellied stove occupied a place just to the side of all those windows.

She heard Lee come in behind her, set down their suitcases, then move through the section of the same open space where a pine dining set stood and into the kitchen to the right.

"Marcie would get mad if she saw your little black book out," he said to Chad as his friend joined them. Lee rounded the L-shaped counter that divided the kitchen from the other rooms, snapped a phone book shut and slipped it into a drawer as if he were right at home.

"Yeah, well," Chad put in a little belatedly, "you know your way around, so take care of it." Then Lee's friend set the mouse cage upon the floor. "I need to take the truck back so I have to get going. Why don't you walk me out and I'll fill you in on the housekeeping details?"

Lee glanced at Blythe as if to make sure she would be all right if he left her alone for a few minutes.

"Go ahead. I need to call Gib and let him know where I am," she said, answering his look.

"The phone is right here," Lee pointed out, sliding it from the kitchen side of the marble counter to the living-dining-room side before he followed his friend.

When they were gone Blythe took a deep breath, glancing around. They'd left her house so suddenly and unexpectedly that she felt as if a tornado had picked her up and set her down in Oz.

Haywire, she thought. Her life had definitely gone haywire.

"I guess you being the best customer of the bakery down the street has its payoffs," Lee said as he and Chad walked down to the van.

"See how lucky you are that I like their pastry for breakfast every morning?"

"So what's the news you said you had when I called to set up the great escape?" Lee asked when they'd reached the delivery truck.

Chad opened the vehicle's door and stood behind it. "I finally talked to Virginia."

Lee was fleetingly aware of a reluctance in himself to hear what the lab assistant had said. He ignored it. Crossing his arms over his chest, he took a step away from Chad and studied the van's tire. "Well, let's hear it."

"It seem that our biochemist was assisting another scientist—a guy named Jerry Nickles—at the time he came up with a diet drink. When he applied for the patent she claimed that she had had an equal part in the discovery and a right to half the patent, licensing fees and profits."

"But she didn't take the formula from him?" Lee wanted to know.

"No, rumor had it that he started to get suspicious of her for some reason and had been using another lab on the last lap, so she wouldn't have access to what he was doing. When he made his breakthrough, the only way she could get her hands in the cookie jar was to make the claim. I guess she figured if she made a big enough stink about it he'd settle out of court and she'd come away with a hefty amount of money. But instead the guy didn't back down. And we know how it turned out. Virginia says Coopersmith was just angling for a fast buck at someone else's expense."

"I thought you said your old girlfriend was a fan of Blythe's?" Lee hadn't intended to speak so sharply.

Chad held up his hands, palms outward. "Don't kill the messenger, Lee. That's what I remembered and I was right. Virginia said that at first she didn't believe what was being said about Coopersmith. But then she actually talked to this Jerry Nickles guy and changed her mind. Besides, if Coopersmith had had any real claim to that diet drink she wouldn't have been ruled against, would she? But she wasn't awarded a thing."

"Which doesn't necessarily mean she was lying. Maybe she just couldn't prove her claim," Lee said, thinking that at the moment Howard was in just that position.

"Come on," Chad cajoled. "If she had contributed anything at all to the work, she would have been able to substantiate it and the court would have given her something—maybe not half of the rights, but surely some compensation. Could be our girl learned from her first mistake, minded her p's and q's with Howard so he wouldn't see through her the way this Nickles guy did, and then walked off with the goods when your uncle had his formula finished."

"She's not that devious." Lee was suddenly aware that he couldn't stop himself from defending her.

"No? Then how do you explain the similarities between then and now?"

"I can't," he admitted. "She just doesn't seem like the type. The more I talk to her, the more I can't help wondering if there isn't some missing piece to this whole mess."

"Like what? That she contributed to Howard's formula so she had some right to take it? I thought your uncle said it was one hundred percent his baby?"

"He did."

"Do you think he's lying?"

"No." Lee leaned back against the side of the van and scowled at the horizon.

"Well, what do you think?" Chad asked, obviously losing patience.

"I don't know. I wish I did. I just haven't found a motive."

"And you're going to keep looking, aren't you?"

"I'd like to know why she did this, yes."

Chad's expression made it clear that he thought Lee was out of his mind. "Will the reason, no matter what it is, change what she's done to your uncle?"

Good question. "I don't know that, either."

Chad didn't say anything for a moment. "Howard is no dummy, Lee."

Lee laughed and glanced at his friend. "Of course he isn't. That goes without saying. And what does it have to do with anything?"

"It's just that Coopersmith must be good at hiding her dark side or she'd never have fooled him. And I doubt he was attracted to her, so he was seeing her more clearly than . . ."

"Than I am," Lee finished for him.

"I'm just saying that if she wasn't damn good at pretending to be a nice, ethical person, she wouldn't have fooled people like Howard and Virginia, who spent more time with her than you have."

"So you figure she's fooling me?"

Chad shrugged. "You know your uncle. You know what kind of person he is. You know he's a great research scientist. You know he doesn't lie. You know the formula is his." Chad paused. "And you know she has it."

Lee wanted to say he also knew Blythe wouldn't have taken it without a damn good reason. But he couldn't. How could he support it? By saying she didn't kiss like a research pirate? "Your point is taken—I shouldn't let myself be blinded by the light."

"Or by turning the lights out—if you know what I mean."

"I get it, Dad—think with what's above my shoulders and not with what's below my belt, right?" Lee said facetiously.

Chad clapped him on the back. "Right. I'm so glad we had this little father-son chat," his friend said, clearly trying to ease the tension the conversation had put between them.

"Yeah, me, too," Lee grumbled. "Any more words of wisdom?"

"Don't swim too soon after a meal and look before you leap."

"What would I do without you?"

"Boggles the mind, doesn't it?" Chad got into the driver's seat. "Keep a cool head."

"And my eyes open at all times." Lee shut the van door.

"No kidding. Don't forget what this mess is doing to your uncle. Even if she has a reason, there must have been a better way of handling it."

Much as he wanted to, Lee couldn't deny that. Instead he said, "Thanks for the help. Have a good weekend."

Chad glanced at the house, then back at Lee. "You, too. Just not too good." He pulled out of the driveway.

Before going back into the house Lee went down to the road to check his mailbox. There were only two envelopes, so he folded them and put them into his pocket. That junk mail he'd left on the counter when he'd been home to pack the other day had been a close call, not to mention the open phone book; if Blythe had happened to get a closer look, the jig would have been up. Remembering that as he headed for the house made him wonder how hard it was going to be to keep Blythe from finding out this was his place.

Taking a mental inventory he realized there were some family pictures on the bureau in his bedroom that he'd better get rid of fast. What else might give him away?

He subscribed to the magazines in the den—they would have labels with his name. And there might be a prescription bottle or two in the bathroom, so they would have to go.

He couldn't think of anything else, but decided he'd better find a way to check every room before Blythe had a chance to notice anything.

Luckily she was still on the phone with her brother. He indicated that he'd give her some privacy, then made a beeline up the four steps, heading for the second level. There wasn't anything in the main bathroom, so he moved on to the den. The magazines went into the filing cabinet beside his drafting table, then he checked his desk for telltale signs. He found nothing, but as he headed out he realized there was a joke trophy on the top shelf of his bookcase. Chad had given it to him on his birthday—Lee Horvat, World's Greatest Lover. Lee retraced his steps and put it away with the magazines.

The two guest bedrooms didn't need checking because he knew there was nothing in them. Instead he went into his own room. He'd packed in a hurry and the evidence was all over the bed and the floor. He scooped up everything and tossed it into the bottom of the closet. From the adjoining bathroom he cleared the medicine chest of a prescription for cough medicine and another for the painkillers that hadn't done anything but put him to sleep when he'd torn the ligaments in his knee last summer. Then he opened the top drawer of the dresser and slid the bottles and the family pictures inside. He just had to hope that she never looked in his closet, because one glance at the length of his pants would tell her his much shorter friend couldn't own them.

Blythe was giving her brother the phone number when Lee went back downstairs. Thinking he was in the clear, he picked up the suitcases he'd set behind the sofa. That was when he saw the photographs on the coffee table. He glanced at Blythe. Her back was to him so he went around the couch, but before he got to the pictures he'd taken of the bridge he'd just finished in Seattle she turned to face him, rolling her eyes at something her brother was saying. Lee smiled at her and hoped he looked nonchalant as he picked up the snapshots and pretended curiosity for a moment before taking them with him when he went back for the bags.

Another close call, he thought as he climbed the stairs to the upper level again. He put Blythe's small suitcase into the bedroom nearest the main bath, then headed to his own room before he realized that might look strange. If either of them was going to have the master bedroom, courtesy dictated that it be Blythe. He veered into the second guest room at the end of the hall. He'd have to be careful of what he did out of habit.

Blythe was off the phone when he went downstairs again. She was standing at the dining-room table, holding up the hem of her T-shirt to a point just below her breasts. Lee's first thought was purely sexual before he realized she was not undressing. She was pulling papers out of the waistband of her jeans.

He stopped on the bottom step. "Should I go back until you call me?" he offered—a split second after he realized those papers she was wearing had to be the formula for EASY.

"No, it's okay," she said as she set them on the table, retrieved the registered letter from the same place, then pulled her shirt down.

Lee closed the space between the stairs and the table. "The formula?"

"The one and only."

"Uh . . . does the fact that you're taking it out in front of me mean you trust me?"

Blythe shrugged. "You've stuck with me through the thick of this. I think you've earned it."

Her trusting him was a giant leap toward getting his hands on Howard's formula. So why did he feel so strange about it? "In that case, could you use a lab assistant?" he offered.

"Sure. You can feed Maude and Hershel," she said, obviously enjoying the suggestion because her eyes took on that glimmer he liked.

Lee moaned but went to the cage, setting it on the counter. "What do they eat?"

"Anything. The more fattening the better."

As he took out the most calorie-laden things he could find, Lee watched Blythe separate the pages of the formula. If she trusted him enough to let him get this close, maybe she'd trust him enough to tell him what she was doing with it. And why she'd taken it from Howard in the first place. "Don't you need beakers and Bunsen burners and microscopes?" he asked.

"Not at the moment," she answered.

So much for that try. He gingerly filled the mice's dish through the bars. "So, this formula is a diet miracle, huh? It must not work too well, or why would these rats be so fat?"

"They haven't had any yet. The point is to beef them up and then give it to them to see if the stuff works."

Lee finished feeding the rodents and took the cage into the mudroom off the kitchen. Then he came back and sat down at the table with Blythe. When she glanced up at him he said, "Your rats stopped eating, so I left their dish full and put them in the other room."

She grinned at him and it tightened things in him that had no business responding like that. "You don't think your friend's fiancée would like mice in her kitchen, or you just couldn't stand the sight of them?"

"Both." Lee pointed to the papers with his chin. "What makes this stuff so great?"

She went back to arranging the pages. "It's a combination of enzymes and chemicals that actually eat calories and fat before the body can absorb them. One dose taken after a two-thousand calorie meal, for instance, should soak up eighteen hundred of those calories, leaving it the same as only having eaten two hundred. Plus it won't alter the body's intake of any of the nutrients."

Lee nodded, knowing she was telling him the truth and realizing her further openness was more ground gained. "If it works it would be worth a fortune," he pointed out, watching closely for her reaction.

She just shrugged. "Sure, but it has more value than money alone. It could put an end to obesity and all the health problems that go along with it, not to mention making life better and easier for everybody who's struggling to keep even small amounts of weight off. And actually, the cost to produce it will be small, so even with a normal markup it will be affordable to everyone, under prescription, of course."

"It would still make enough for you to retire to the Bahamas."

She wrinkled her nose. "No, thanks."

"You don't like the Bahamas?"

"I've never been there. But it doesn't matter. I love what I do. I wouldn't want to stop."

"Even if you were so rich you never had to work another day in your life?"

"Money has never been that big of a deal to me."

There wasn't anything in her tone to make him think otherwise. But if money—either the desire or the need for it—wasn't why she took EASY, what was the reason?

Lee watched her search for a pencil in her purse and scribble something along the border of one page. "I hate to touch on a sore subject, but everything I've heard seems to hold that this formula is finished," he said in a hurry, alarmed to see for himself that she was actually amending Howard's notes.

"They all do seem to think that, don't they?" she answered vaguely as she went on writing.

Why was she amending those notes? Was it some feeble attempt to put her own stamp on it? Maybe she was trying to increase or decrease the strength of the drug. Whatever the purpose, she did seem to be tampering with his uncle's work. When she crossed out a line of Howard's writing, Lee's concern mounted.

"Is there something else I can do?" he said, trying to distract her.

She only shook her head and said, "No. Thanks, anyway," without even looking up from the papers.

That didn't give him many options. Lee got up from the table and went around the counter into the kitchen, where he could keep an eye on what she was doing over her shoulders. At least she was only using pencil and putting a single line through what she was deleting. As far as he could tell she hadn't done anything that left Howard's notes obliterated. But who could tell what she might do? At any given moment she could destroy whole parts of the formula.

That prospect made him very edgy. Had it not been for her enthusiasm when she talked about the benefits of EASY, he'd have thought she was sabotaging it.

He considered trying to strong-arm the notes away from her, then discarded the idea. Not only was it unappealing, but the possibility of damaging the papers prohibited it.

He thought about interrupting her repeatedly just to keep her from working on them. But what if she got aggravated and secluded herself and EASY, the way she had at her house?

In the end he decided to ply her with liquids. The first trip to the bathroom and he'd grab the formula.

For three hours that was just what Lee did, all the while watching her every move. But when she finally got up to answer the call of nature she took three pages with her and thwarted his plan. He couldn't chance the loss or damage of those pages so he just stood at the table, looking at that formula, which might as well have been written in Greek, for all he could decipher.

The only hope he had left was that in her newfound trust of him she would let him know where she hid the formula when she put it away for the day. And in the meantime all he could do was watch helplessly as she wrote on and deleted things from page after page of what was Howard's best work.

Just before five Blythe threw her pencil onto the table and let out a subdued shriek.

"Trouble?" Lee asked.

She closed her eyes and dropped her head back. "Nothing makes sense. Everything is a blur. My brain is clogged," she groaned in mock agony, pulling her hair. "And I'm so-o-o frustrated."

At least he wasn't alone. And if she was frustrated, maybe that meant that whatever she was trying to do with the formula wasn't working. "You know, when I was in college and I'd hit a wall in trying to study or figure out a problem, it always helped me to put it away and forget about it for awhile. It is Saturday, after all, and this week has been a tough one. Maybe you ought to give yourself tonight and tomorrow to relax and not think about work. Monday you can get a fresh start with a clear head." At this point anything, no matter how unlikely it was that she'd agree, was worth a try.

"There's only one problem with that idea," she said.

"Which is?"

"My brother is paying you for your time. It's bad enough that I wasted yesterday using your plumbing talents. I can't waste more than that."

Lee sat down at the table across from her once more. "What if I don't charge him for my services again until Monday?"

She gave him a dubious frown. "Wouldn't the Executive Protection Agency have your head for something like that?"

"I think I can get around them."

"But is it a good idea?"

He shrugged. "Seems like a great one to me." And if he was honest with himself, he had to admit that it really did seem like a great idea to spend some leisure time with Blythe.

Blythe turned her head toward the living room, then glanced at him out of the corner of one eye. "Just you and me?"

"Unless you'd like the media invited," he teased.

"I don't know if it's wise," she said, plainly more to herself than to him.

He purposely misunderstood. "Inviting the media is definitely not wise."

She seemed to be thinking about it, and Lee had the feeling that the formula wasn't what she was using as a gauge. She caught her bottom lip between her teeth and he knew she was feeling tempted.

"Come on," he coaxed.

She took a deep breath that raised her breasts in a way he was all too aware of. "I shouldn't, but I know myself well enough to realize that time out will do me more good than harm, so I'll be more productive in the long run."

It was genuine pleasure that made Lee smile. "Does that mean we're on?"

Again she hesitated, looking as if she knew she shouldn't give in. Then she smiled back at him, if a little tentatively. "Okay. We're on."

"Terrific." And he meant it.

"I don't suppose you know of a good hiding place around here?"

That took him by surprise. "For the formula?"

"And the registered letter."

Lee didn't answer right away. She was dropping EASY into his lap and he couldn't believe it. But some other niggling feeling was keeping his disbelief company. Something he couldn't quite pin down. "As a matter of fact," he said a little slowly, "there's a secret panel I know about in the den."

"Secret panel?" She laughed.

"I know it sounds strange, but it's there."

"And you think it's safe?"

"Sure," he retorted, wondering at himself.

"Okay, let's take a look."

She stood up and gathered the papers into a pile. The sound of her bouncing the edges against the table to straighten them seemed especially loud. Why had he felt better about this when she hadn't trusted him?

"The den is next to the bathroom, isn't it?" she asked, interrupting his introspection.

"Yeah. I'll show you," he said, still distracted by his own oddly warring emotions.

"At home," she informed him as she followed, "I rolled everything up and hid it in the shower rod. But there isn't one on the bathtub upstairs."

"So that was your hiding place," he said, coming back to himself. "I wondered."

The panel was in the bookcase, concealed behind a seven-inch-high dictionary. The previous owners of the house had shown it to Lee but at the time he'd thought it was silly, that he'd never have a use for it.

Then the formula and the registered letter were inside the brick-sized hole, the panel was back in place, and so was the dictionary.

"Well, I guess that's done," she said. She sounded a little uneasy and Lee wondered if she sensed that she'd just lost the game. But she simply turned on her heel and headed for the door. "I think I could use a long, hot bubble bath in that marble tub."

"Good idea," Lee agreed as he followed her out of the room. "And while you're at it I'll see what we can cook for dinner."

She crossed the hall to her room and he went down-stairs, as if he didn't have anything on his mind but checking the refrigerator. It wasn't until he heard the water turned on in the bathroom that he climbed the stairs to the den again.

He closed the door and went right to the bookcase; for a moment, he stared at that dictionary without moving it. Then, very deliberately, because his fingers had stiffened up on him, he took it down and opened the panel. And there it was, Howard's formula, wrapped around Blythe's registered letter to herself.

What now? he asked himself as he held the precious pages in his hand.

He could walk out while she was in the tub, and this whole thing would be over. That was probably what he should do.

But he didn't want to.

However much he had wanted and needed to get EASY back, he wanted and needed this time with Blythe.

Why was that?

Because he'd come to care for her, he realized suddenly, feeling like a traitor.

But the formula was safe now. He could lock it up where she couldn't possibly get her hands on it. And that being the case, would any harm be done by indulging himself a little? After all, Howard was gone until Monday, anyway, without even access to a phone.

Taking the formula down to the garage and locking it in the trunk of his car, Lee couldn't help wondering if he was just asking for trouble by not getting behind the wheel and driving away. After all, the more time he spent with her, the better he got to know her, the deeper went the roots of his feelings.

But at that moment it didn't make any difference to him.

He'd done what he'd set out to. Now he needed a little time just for himself.

Besides, if he left now he'd never find out what her motive was. He'd never know if she had a good reason for taking EASY. A reason that justified what she'd put Howard through. A reason that made it all right for Lee to be falling in love with her.

Chapter Seven

Trust was on Blythe's mind as she soaked in the big oval tub. It wasn't that she hadn't trusted Lee from the first time they'd met; after all, he'd been hired to move into her house and protect her. But she certainly hadn't considered being open with him about the formula. Until today.

When and how had that changed?

A part of it had come from spending so much time with him in the past few days. Admittedly she still didn't know a lot about him, but she did think she had a pretty good idea of the kind of person he was. And watching him handle Howard so kindly the night before had seemed like evidence that he was one of the good guys, she thought as she slid a little lower in the bubbles that went nearly to the rim of the marble tub.

What had really sold her on Lee's loyalty was his response to the slings and arrows aimed at her in the last twenty-four hours. Sticking with her through the thick and thin of this mess without passing judgment had gone a long way in convincing her she could let down her guard. Somehow, after this morning, realizing that she'd so completely and unquestioningly put herself into his hands to get away from the media madhouse, it had seemed silly for her to go on hiding the formula from him, especially in a place he knew better than she did.

Blythe closed her eyes and let the steamy water relax her. She hadn't realized how tense she'd been until her muscles began to loosen. No wonder she'd been having such a hard time understanding Howard's notes. Lee was right; it had been a tough week and it was adversely affecting her work. Taking some time off to regroup was just the ticket.

But should she give that time to Lee, when she was finding it harder and harder not to like him?

Whom was she kidding? She already liked him. A lot.

A better question to ask herself was whether she should give him that time, when she was beginning to more than like him.

Why was she fighting it? All of a sudden that seemed as ridiculous as hiding the formula from him had. This attraction, this relationship, was happening whether the circumstances were good or not, whether she had scheduled it or not, whether she was charging headlong into it or not. So maybe she should just roll with events. After all, how many times did fate put someone into her path who offered her all he did?

Never before now was the answer. Certainly Jerry Nickles hadn't fitted the bill, regardless of what she'd thought at the beginning of her relationship with him. Unless, of course, the best fate had to offer was a man for whom she had to be a totally self-sacrificing hand-maiden.

She simply didn't believe that was the best fate had to offer her.

Lee seemed like one of the few good men around—like her brother and her father—and she'd be crazy to go on denying what was developing between them, just because he'd come into her life during a particularly rough patch. Especially when that rough patch didn't seem to bother him.

A knock on the bathroom door made her open her eyes.

"Did you drown in there?" Lee called.

"No, I'm still afloat."

"Listen, there's nothing around here to eat, so how about if I buy you dinner?"

Blythe smiled at the prospect. "Sounds good to me. I'll be out in a few minutes."

With bells on.

The restaurant Lee took Blythe to was a small steak house in the business section of Genesee Park. He had assured her that the only clothes she'd packed—jeans and T-shirts—were acceptable attire for the place. He'd even changed from his slacks to jeans to make her more comfortable. But not until Blythe saw for herself as they went into the place that there were other people casually dressed did she relax. The black V-necked top with bright flowers embroidered above her left breast like a broach was not out of order among people wearing designer sweat suits and tennis outfits. In fact, with her hair left in a natural cascade of curls to her shoulders and the faint eye shadow she'd applied, she fitted right in.

The hostess seated them in a booth along one of the paneled walls in the dimly lighted restaurant and handed them menus chalk-written on slates. There were people at most of the other tables, but the place was still quiet and cozy.

"They have a filet served with béarnaise that's to die for," Lee informed her before even looking at his menu.

"You must come here often. The hostess seemed to recognize you and now you even know what to order without looking."

"Chad and I come whenever I'm up here to see him. Something about this near-mountain air makes me meat-and-potatoes-hungry."

Blythe intended to take his suggestion, but pretended to look at the menu, all the while studying him surreptitiously as he looked over his. He'd showered while she was dressing and there was a fresh-scrubbed look about him that was very appealing. The sea-green polo shirt he wore molded itself to his broad shoulders like a second skin. His hair was combed, he'd shaved, and the now-familiar scent of his cologne wafted across the table to cause small stirrings in her every time she caught a whiff of it. All in all, Blythe decided, she couldn't care less what she ate as long as she got to be with him while she ate it.

The waitress came to bring the wine Lee had ordered for them and memorize their dinner selections. When she left Lee picked up the keys he'd set on the table as they'd been seated. "I don't suppose I could persuade you to put these in your purse, could I? Tight jeans are hell for carrying keys, and if I leave them on the table I'll forget them."

Blythe took the plain gold ring and dropped it into her black leather bucket bag, having a much too vivid mental image of just how tight his jeans were over the muscles of his thighs and across his perfect rear end.

"Are you sure your friend won't care that we took his car out?" she asked to distract herself from the thought of his body.

"It's his pride and joy," Lee said of the fancy English sports coupé. "But he told me before he left that we could use it." Then Lee changed the subject. "You look like you feel better after your long bath," he observed, watching her with those aquamarine eyes, the color of what Blythe imagined the waters of Hawaii to be.

She sipped her wine and smiled. "Did I look bad before?"

He smiled back at her and for the first time she noticed how straight and white his teeth were. "You didn't look bad, no. Just frazzled."

"I was frazzled. I just didn't realize it."

"But you're better now?"

"Much." Their salads came and as Blythe peppered hers she said, "If I'm out in left field it's because my only knowledge of bodyguards comes from TV, but are you a detective, too?"

He finished chewing his bite of salad, then gave her a half grin. "Why, do you need something detected?"

"No, I just wondered."

"I'm not a detective, no."

"Do you make a good living as a bodyguard? I mean, not that I'm being nosy, it's just that your friend made that comment about earning more with his bakery..."

"It's okay. I do all right, but I feel the way you said you did about money—it isn't the most important thing in my life, either."

"What is?"

"The people in it. My family and friends," he answered truthfully.

Being close to her own family, that was something Blythe was happy to hear. It always rubbed her the wrong way to meet people who carried around adolescent baggage about their parents' or siblings' shortcomings. "Where do you live when you're not bodyguarding?" she asked then, wanting some background scenery to put behind her visualization of him.

But the waitress came at that moment to take their salad dishes and replace them with sizzling steaks and baked potatoes. When she left, Lee picked up the wine bottle. "Your glass is almost empty," he said as he refilled it and then poured himself another.

When he didn't say anything else Blythe assumed he'd forgotten she'd asked him a question. She hated to repeat it so tried a different tack. "I know you were born and raised in Colorado, but have you lived here your whole adult life, too?"

"With the exception of a few months here and there. Have you?"

"Always." She took a bite of her steak. "You were right, this is wonderful," she said when she'd swallowed it.

He looked pleased and that was all it took for him to win a point in comparison with Jerry Nickles, who had never cared whether or not she liked his choice of restaurants.

"When we're finished," he said between bites, "we'll order their house speciality for dessert—homemade peppermint ice cream. I know, it sounds crazy, but it's the perfect finale."

After tasting her potato Blythe went on with her quest, still hoping he'd offer more about himself. "Have you ever wanted to live anywhere else?"

He shook his head. "I love the change of seasons. I'd hate to be somewhere that was virtually the same climate year round—good or bad."

Another point in Lee's favor. Jerry Nickles had always thought her provincial because she wanted to stay in Colorado. "I wouldn't mind someplace with summers a little cooler than here, but other than that I feel the same way."

"If you're bothered by the heat you just need to move out of the heart of Denver. Genesee, for instance, is perfect—close enough to everything to be convenient, but far enough into the mountains to cut a few degrees off the hottest days."

"You must spend a lot of time up here with your friend."

For some reason that seemed to make him pause. "Yes, I guess you could say that. I really like Genesee."

"Do you live far from here?"

"No, not far." He held out the basket of bread. "You have to try these French rolls. They're baked here fresh every day."

Blythe made a face. "I don't suppose you'd consider splitting one with me, would you? I'm already getting full."

He agreed and she broke the crusty roll in half, unable to keep from grinning as she did.

"What?" he asked. "Is sharing a dinner roll funny?"

"I was just thinking that this is sort of a first date. Ordinarily on a first date I would have either refused the roll or taken one, eaten half myself and just left the rest.

The familiarity of sharing food wouldn't happen until much later.''

The laugh lines around his eyes crinkled. "I didn't know there was a schedule for these things. How many dates does it usually take before you share food?"

She thought about it for a minute. "I don't think I should answer that."

"Why not?"

"Because it would give away how little I date."

"What does that mean? That you never get far enough to do it?"

She definitely never got far enough to do it, she thought, but managed to resist the temptation to make a reply to the double meaning she'd taken from his phrasing. "I can safely say that you are only the second unrelated man I've ever shared food with."

"No?"

"Sad to say."

"Then I feel honored."

"Doesn't take much to thrill you, does it?" she teased him.

"Oh, I don't know," he said, grinning back at her.

The waitress interrupted them to ask how their meals were and when she'd gone, Lee glanced at Blythe from under his strong brows, one of them devilishly arched. "So how long has it been since you shared food with an unrelated man?" he asked with a sparkle in his eyes that told her he had double meanings on his mind, too.

"Five years."

"Five years," he repeated. "Seems like a lot of things date back to then."

This time it was Blythe who ignored the comment, putting her hand over her wineglass when he moved to refill it yet again. "No more for me, thanks."

When he'd topped his own glass, Lee put down the bottle and settled those piercing eyes on her again. "Five years since your professional life fell apart. Five years since your last and only serious relationship. Five years since you've... shared food with a man. I'd sure like to know what happened five years ago."

Blythe wrinkled her nose. "You don't want to hear my war stories," she said as she pushed her plate away.

"Funny, I thought I did. It seems to me that knowing where this other guy went wrong will keep me off the same path."

She pulled her wineglass in front of her plate and stared at her thumb, which was running across the flowers beveled into the side of the glass. "I don't think there's much chance of you taking the same path, anyway. It was a pretty convoluted one."

"And it mixed business with pleasure, and taught you to avoid that combination," he observed, paraphrasing what she'd told him before. "Everything you've said about it only makes me more curious. What was this guy? A fellow biochemist who had a plot to overthrow the free world, with you playing Bonnie to his Clyde?"

That made her smile. "Not quite."

"What then?"

"You're really determined to hear this tonight, aren't you?"

"Absolutely."

Blythe considered whether or not to spill the sordid details of her life while their ice cream was served. As always with Lee she had the feeling that he was genuinely interested in her. And since she'd adopted this new openness with him, why stop now? Maybe it would inspire the same from him.

"His name was Jerry Nickles," she began. "He was a part of the university's research department, too. He worked with one group of chemists who were looking into new forms of diet pills, and I was with a different group, exploring some possibilities with high-fiber caramels that expand in the stomach before a meal to prevent overeating of higher-calorie foods. But everybody would brainstorm together and after awhile he and I started to realize how good we were at tossing ideas back and forth, even when the rest of the people we worked with weren't around. Anyway, he wanted to leave the structure of the CU lab and start his own group and he asked me to join him."

"Was this before or after you'd started the personal relationship?"

"I was attracted to him before, but we didn't actually start dating until after I'd thrown in with him professionally. We put our separate knowledge and experience together and started work on a liquid diet drink. Long hours turned into late dinners and things just snowballed from there. Within six months he had moved into my house. A year after that we made a breakthrough in our research."

"Sounds promising."

"That's what I thought, too. But it was the beginning of the end—not that I knew it at the time."

"What happened?"

She shrugged. "We were pretty far along in our research—in fact I thought we were close to coming up with a viable product—when we seemed to hit a wall and every experiment started to fail. That sometimes happens so I took it in my stride, but Jerry didn't seem to be able to—or so I interpreted his sudden withdrawal from me—personally and professionally. I thought he was down in the dumps because things were going wrong. Even so, I wasn't crazy about his new need for space, for time alone, for nights out by himself...." Blythe passed Lee the remainder of her ice cream when he finished his and she couldn't eat any more. "I started to think he was having an affair."

"Was he?"

"In a way," she said wryly. "He was having an affair with the facilities at another lab. Apparently he let our work go just far enough to see in what direction success was likely to be found, and from then on he sabotaged what we were doing together and reproduced the experiments on his own when he could sneak away. When he came up with a successful product, he moved out and filed for the patent in his name alone."

Lee set down his spoon and pushed away what remained of her dessert. Leaning back in the booth, he laid one forearm on the table, drawing a water ring with his index finger. "You hadn't protected yourself?" he asked without looking at her.

Blythe couldn't help a dry laugh at that. "Personally there's no way to protect yourself from another person's secret agenda when it doesn't include you. But professionally I thought I was covered, albeit a little late. At that point in my life I tended to pay more attention to the work than to details. Unfortunately—or stupidly—when we finally got around to writing the letter that dated our idea I made a big mistake. After we'd written it together, naming us as cocreators of the concept for the diet drink, I went back to work and Jerry took the letter to be witnessed and sent to us by registered mail. I didn't see any problem with that because, of course, I trusted him. I was living with him, for crying out loud. We were talking about getting married."

Blythe paused while the waitress asked if there would be anything else and left the bill.

"Go on," Lee prompted after the woman left.

"When he moved out I still didn't have a clue about what he'd done. He said he just wasn't sure about our relationship anymore, or what he wanted. He couldn't make a commitment—the usual breaking-up stuff. I asked where that left us professionally and he said he needed some time to sort that out. Two days after he'd gone a mutual friend told me he'd filed for a solo patent on the diet drink. I was stunned, of course. I called an attorney who advised me to file a claim for half. I did. It went to court, the letter was opened and—lo and behold—I was nowhere in it. Apparently he'd trashed the letter that gave me my share of the credit for the idea and replaced it with one that only listed his name, witnessed and everything."

"You couldn't prove you'd done the work?" Lee asked solemnly.

She shook her head. "We were the only two people working in his lab. Jerry insisted that my claim was sour grapes over the end of our personal relationship, and with the witnessed letter and postmarked envelope I was sunk."

Lee frowned down at his after-dinner coffee. "Do you think he'd planned to steal your work right from the start?"

"It's impossible to say. All I know for sure is that I felt like an idiot." She laughed a small, mirthless laugh at herself. "But hey, it was one of those learning experiences everyone likes to think are worth the agony they go through to get."

He studied her with an unwavering gaze. "What did it teach you?"

"To watch out for myself," she said, laughing genuinely this time. "I'll tell you one thing. No matter how dumb an idea I come up with, I write it down, have it witnessed and send it to myself by registered mail. And I would never, ever, leave it up to anyone else to do again, that's for sure."

"Do you have a lot of ideas—dumb or otherwise?"

She shrugged. "Sure. I'm working on my fourth large-size safety deposit box already."

That made him smile. "You're kidding."

"Nope. My poor mailman must think I'm some kind of nut with all the registered letters I send to myself."

Leaving the money with the bill, Lee slid out of the booth and reached a hand to help Blythe do the same. She didn't need help, but took his hand, anyway. It was warm and big and hers slipped into it as if it were meant to be there.

"So that was when your life fell apart," Lee said as they left the restaurant.

He kept on holding her hand even after she was out of the booth and Blythe was thinking more about the skitter of sensations running up her arm. It took her a moment to get with the program again. "Claiming what appeared to be another scientist's idea and work turned me into an instant pariah," she explained once they were in the car and headed home. "Credibility, respect, the chance to work with other researchers, let alone a group, the possibility of getting funding—all went out the window before I could sneeze. That was where Howard stepped in," she finished, aware that her voice had grown a little softer.

"As I recall, you said he took you in when no one else would."

Blythe smiled at him. It felt good to know Lee had not only listened so intently to all she'd said to him in these past few days, but had thought enough about it—or her—to retain it. "I had only seen Howard a couple of times between when he and I both left CU and when all this happened to me. But when he heard about it he came to my rescue. It took guts on his part and cost him a couple of good scientists who refused to work with me."

Even in profile she saw the frown that pulled at Lee's features. She knew he was wondering how she could have come from a time when Howard had been the only person to believe in her to what was going on now. And she wanted to explain it to him. But she couldn't. There were other loyalties she owed. So instead she said, "And there you have my war story. Did it give you indigestion?"

He didn't answer her right away and she knew he was weighing whether or not to pursue the part of his curiosity that she'd left unsatisfied. When he stopped at a red light just then he glanced at her, his expression more troubled than she'd at first realized from his profile.

Before he could ask she shook her head and stopped him. "I can't talk about any more of it."

He smiled a little but it didn't reach his eyes. "Why? Are you a spy on a top-secret mission? Or is a rival faction holding Maude and Hershel's mother captive until you do their dirty work for them?"

"It's personal," Blythe said.

"You owe a loan shark a million dollars that you have to pay up right now or he's going to throw you in the Colorado River with your feet in cement shoes?" he guessed again, his voice edged with a more serious tone than his words conveyed.

"Not quite."

"Am I even close?"

"Not even."

"And you can't talk about it," he repeated.

"Right."

For a moment more he went on staring at her as if trying to read the answers in her face. Then he looked
straight ahead again, lifting both of his hands from the
steering wheel in a show of deference to her wishes.
"Okay," he said amiably.

Oh, yes, she liked this man a lot. "Thanks."

"For what?"

"For everything. But mostly for not judging or thinking too harshly of me." She laughed. "Or at least for not
showing it, if you do think I'm a horrible person."

There was a short silence before he glanced at her
again, the frown still putting lines between his eyes. "I
don't think you're a horrible person," he said as if he
meant it.

Blythe smiled, more pleased to hear it than she could
tell him. "It wouldn't surprise me if you did. But I didn't
think you considered me the world's biggest creep, since
you always make me feel that you're giving me the benefit of the doubt. Or at least trying to."

"I am."

"It means a lot to me. And as I said before, what I've
done isn't as bad as it seems," she said quietly.

As Lee turned into the driveway he pushed the button
on a control hooked to the visor and the garage door
opened automatically so he could pull in. Getting out of
the car ended the conversation that Blythe was only too
willing to have done with.

"Oh, look at that view!" she exclaimed as they went
into the house, noticing the spots of light that marked
Denver's skyline through the wall of windows in the living room.

Lee stopped short of turning the lights on, leaving the house dark. "It is pretty spectacular. But it's even better from the deck," he said, going to the sliding door in the dining room, opening it and waiting for Blythe to go out before him.

She didn't need any more of an invitation than that. The spring air was cool and pine scented. There were no streetlights, and those from the nearest house down the hill were too far away to be more than square specks in the distance. With the house dark behind them the white and gold city lights were bright enough to form a hazy halo around the clustered buildings.

She stood with both of her hands on the redwood banister that bordered the deck, staring straight out at the city and imagining the bustle there on a Saturday night as people met friends, danced, drank, went to the theater or the symphony or crowded into a live jazz performance. She felt far removed from it all, but thought that given any of those choices, she'd choose to be right where she was, with Lee.

He joined her, but instead of looking at the view he propped a hip on the top rail and angled her way.

Blythe felt him studying her and sensed that their earlier discussion had left some lingering questions he was having trouble shaking. Nonetheless she felt so comfortable with him, so confident that he wasn't thinking ill of her that neither his scrutiny nor his suddenly quiet mood disturbed her.

"This is just what I needed," she said, closing her eyes and breathing in the special smell of mountain air. Then she put her side to the railing, leaning an elbow there, and met Lee eye to eye. "We always seem to talk about me. Why don't you tell me about you, for a change?"

Moonlight barely dusted his features enough for her to see him smile with only one corner of his mouth. "What do you want to know?"

Blythe thought about that for a moment. She wanted to know everything. The question was where to start. "You told me there isn't anyone special in your life right now and that there hasn't been for a long time. How long?"

The other corner of his mouth arched upward. "A few years," he answered in a slow, smoky voice.

"And was that relationship very serious?"

"Fairly."

"But it ended."

He gave her a full-out grin. "Not as traumatically as yours did."

"Then it was amicable? Just a matter of irreconcilable differences?"

"Yes."

Blythe took a deep breath and sighed with as much exaggeration as she could. "You are very frustrating," she told him.

"Why is that?"

"Because you're giving me the equivalent of name, rank and serial number without really telling me anything. I bared my soul about what happened to me five years ago and you're still playing mystery man."

He held her eyes with his. "A split second before you started to ask about this, I decided that for the rest of tonight I wanted to leave everything—especially the past, yours and mine—out of this evening and only concentrate on you and what I'm feeling about you and this particular moment out of time."

This particular moment out of time. She liked that. It gave her a feeling of having a little distance from what was shadowing her. "Okay," she agreed. He kept staring at her without saying anything, so she turned back to savor the sight of the city lights.

For awhile they stayed just like that, in companionable silence. Then Lee reached a hand to the back of her neck, kneading slightly.

"I like your hair loose," he said in a tone that was deeper than any she'd heard from him, and so low it was barely more than a whisper.

"It usually gets in the way," Blythe responded; she didn't know what else to say to a comment that was a compliment, yet wasn't.

"In the way of what?" he wondered out loud in that same dark-whiskey tone as he rubbed the back of her head.

"It gets in the way of work," she answered, a little weakly; she was thinking more about his touch than his question.

"There are more things in life than work, you know."

Only too well, she thought. There was Lee and the tingle of her scalp beneath his hand, the warmth that radiated from his big body, and the feelings alive in her since she'd met him. Feelings that hadn't been awake in five years. That were not only alive at that moment but dancing a jig in her stomach. And lower. But the conversation was about her hair, she reminded herself. "It gets in the way when I do anything that makes me look down, too," Blythe informed him distractedly. It was the only thing she could think of to say, and she was afraid of what would happen when the talking stopped.

He slid his fingers through her hair to the ends, then brought his hand to cup her chin and turn her face toward him. "But it's nice at times like this."

She started to say, "Times like what?" but never got the words out, because he leaned forward and touched her mouth with his. Blythe had never had a kiss as light as that one, a bare meeting of his parted lips over hers. But like two live wires, that was all it took to set off sparks in her.

He slipped his hand from her chin around to the back of her head again, bringing her closer, deepening the kiss. He tasted of peppermint, better than the ice cream itself. His velvet tongue came slowly in to meet hers and Blythe welcomed it, tip to tip for a moment, before he nudged her mouth open wider and began to explore the edges of her teeth, the soft inside of her lips.

It struck her as strange how instantly they were in sync, as if they'd been at this for years and years, as if each knew the rhythm of the other. It felt so perfect. So right. So wonderful.

He put his free arm around her, pulling her very close, pressing her head back into his hand. Her breasts made their first contact with his chest, and more of those sparks flittered into life, turning both crests hard. She raised her hands to his biceps, solid mounds of muscle that moved and flexed against her palms, his skin beneath the band of his short-sleeved shirt taut and silky and warm.

He opened his mouth wider and so did Blythe, hungry for as much of him as she could have, standing there on the deck with so many clothes between them. He teased her tongue with his and she took the challenge, chasing it back to learn the textures of those straight white teeth of his.

Blythe arched her back to be still closer to him and he answered by holding her tighter. His mouth left hers only to come back again, sucking first her upper lip and then her lower before finding her chin with exploring kisses that went to the sensitive underside, the arch of her throat, the hollow. He moved his hand from the back of her head to the side of her neck, then trailed it to her shoulder, taking her shirt with it, slipping down the V to bare it to him. He kissed and nibbled his way across her collarbone to the exposed inch of her upper arm, tracing feathery strokes there with his tongue.

Blythe couldn't help the almost audible moan that echoed in her throat as he trailed the edge of her crooked neckline with his tongue, leaving a damp path to dry in the cool night air and make her aware of how hot was her skin.

Close, he came so close to her breast without actually touching it, the agony of wanting him was intense. She swallowed with some difficulty and whispered, "That's so nice."

He followed that same line of her shirt with his fingers then, curling them inside as he came slowly nearer to where Blythe wanted him. That first brush of his hand against her breast was like an explosion for her, white-hot and wonderful, leaving her wondering how she had lived without the touch of this man who seemed to have been created especially for her, body and soul.

He kneaded her breast, first on the outside of her shirt and then—blissfully—underneath, filling his considerable palm. Then he explored with his fingers, using their tips to outline her nipples, to flick against their hardness, to tenderly pinch and send a shaft of pure need straight down her middle to the core of her.

This should be happening in bed, she thought. A split second later she realized what both her mind and her body were wanting. No, more than wanting—craving, straining for.

A lot had happened in the past twenty-four hours. They'd come a long way fast. Maybe too fast. Was she absolutely sure she wanted this relationship to go this far already?

Blythe pushed away from Lee with a groan of disappointment that made plain how difficult it was for her. "I think we better slow this down," she managed to say in a weak voice.

He took his hand away from her breast, and Blythe knew the devastating frustration of ending something that felt much, much too good. Then he dropped his head to the top of hers.

"You're probably right," he muttered, grinding out the words in a gravelly voice, just when she was about to reconsider.

Blythe took a deep breath and held it, fighting for some control.

Lee slipped her shirt back into place and kept both of his hands firmly on her shoulders, kneading them in much the same way he had her breast only moments before and unknowingly increasing Blythe's agony. She exhaled that held breath as if deflating, closed her eyes and willed away the desire to have those hands where they'd do her more good.

"Go lock yourself in your room before I lose my grip, Coopersmith," he ordered, turning her toward the sliding glass door and giving her a careful push.

Blythe knew she had to take herself out of there or give in to the intensity of her urges. She went in and closed the screen before turning back to him. "Thanks for dinner..." she said, letting her voice trail off in a way that thanked him for after dinner, too.

It took him a moment to answer and looking at his stiff silhouette she knew he was still fighting a battle with his own desires. Then he nodded and said, "Sure. Anytime."

Blythe couldn't remember anything she'd wanted more than to go back out onto that deck and into his arms. But she told herself it wasn't wise. Not yet, anyway, when as recently as yesterday she hadn't even been willing to let him know about her past.

"Good night," she said, stepping away from the door and hoping distance would break the pull of all she felt for him.

"Good night," he answered.

Blythe made her way through the dark house to her room, where she closed the door, then fell back against it.

Even though she realized that she still didn't know much more about his life than she had before, she couldn't help thinking that maybe Lee was fate's compensation for what she'd been through five years ago.

Chapter Eight

Standing at his rain-streaked bedroom window, Lee watched Sunday dawn under heavy, ash-colored clouds. He'd already been downstairs and made a pot of coffee, and the steam from a mug of it spiraled around his stubbled chin. But it wasn't the weather that was on his mind as he stared out. He was thinking about the same thing that had puzzled him once he'd overcome the blinding desire for Blythe the night before: the discrepancy between her story about what had happened to her five years ago and Chad's.

Wondering if he was a fool, Lee admitted to himself that he believed Blythe's version. It made more sense to him that she would have taken her claim on the diet drink all the way to court only if it was valid and she had contributed to the formulation. A legal battle to appropriate a portion of another researcher's work just didn't seem worth the trouble, given her lack of evidence.

So where did that leave him—in terms of Blythe's motives? She'd been cheated by a man she'd trusted and cared about. That kind of betrayal had to have left scars, even if she didn't show them.

Had it also left her with the feeling that being victimized by a man who was close to her gave her the right to victimize someone else? Had it left her with an every-scientist-for-himself philosophy? Did she think that having lost out on the profits and benefits of what she had genuinely contributed to justified taking Howard's formula as compensation?

Those were all possibilities Lee couldn't overlook. And they grew stronger when he considered the similarities between what Jerry Nickles had done to her and what she'd done to Howard. Hadn't this Nickles guy been a close and trusted part of her life, just as Blythe had been a close and trusted peer of Howard's? Hadn't his uncle been less than conscientious about protecting his work with the registered letter, opening the way to a similar opportunity for someone else to claim EASY? And even now, wasn't Blythe doing something with the formula behind Howard's back, much the way Nickles had finished the work on the diet drink? In fact, all in all, the two situations couldn't be more alike.

Except for one thing.

Blythe.

She just didn't seem to be the kind of person who could do what Nickles had. She didn't seem to be carrying a grudge. She didn't seem to have the attitude that if someone had done it to her, she had the right to do it to someone else. Not even in telling her story had she sounded bitter.

That left Lee again wondering if Blythe had taken the formula for EASY out of some kind of necessity. Except that she'd denied every possibility he'd proposed as the reason for it. Maybe he just hadn't guessed right. And she had said that what she'd done wasn't as bad as it seemed.

Well, it was an indisputable fact that she'd taken Howard's formula, and that seemed pretty damn bad. She'd sent herself a registered letter naming the creator of the idea. She was doing everything she could to keep his uncle from reclaiming EASY. How could any of that not be as bad as it seemed?

And yet...

Lee hadn't been lying when he'd told her he was giving her the benefit of the doubt. Maybe it was just plain blind hope that something he didn't yet know would turn this mess around and make everything all right.

But, blind or not, he couldn't help hoping. Because none of what he'd come up with so far felt right—not Blythe as a habitual research pirate, not Blythe as the victim becoming the victimizer, not Blythe as a greedy, glory-seeking villainess, not Blythe as an unwilling thief pressed into stealing by extreme circumstances.

So what did feel right?

Blythe in his arms was the only answer he could come up with.

Nothing had felt more right than that. Not for a long, long time.

Lee had a broom handle stuck in the drain of the kitchen sink when Blythe went downstairs that morning. The sleeves of his yellow sport shirt were rolled to the elbows, the tendons of his forearms bulged and his hands gripped the broomstick like an oarsman's; he was obviously trying to unjam the garbage disposal.

"Playing plumber again?" she asked as she rounded the marble counter.

"Afraid so," he answered, taking the broom handle out of the sinkhole and bending over to push the Reset button on the disposal underneath.

Blythe didn't mean to stare at his rear end, in blue jeans that were slightly looser than those he'd worn before, but somehow she just couldn't help it. And even when she told herself to look somewhere else, her gaze stayed glued to those two back pockets as she thought that she preferred him in the tighter-fitting denims.

Lee straightened up, turned on the water and flicked the switch that started the disposal. When it roared to life he threw her a self-satisfied smile.

"Bingo," he said. Then he put the broom into a closet whose oak door matched the rest of the cupboards and turned back to Blythe. "Good morning."

She glanced out the window at the rain. "I think it is, but I'm usually the only one to appreciate weather like this."

"I love an occasional rainy day. What shall we do with it?"

What Blythe wanted to do with it was stay here in this cozy house alone with Lee. Lying on the floor in front of a fire. In his arms. Naked.

"If I wasn't a fugitive I'd go into downtown Denver. I didn't realize how long it's been since I was there until we drove through yesterday," she said, trying to outrun her thoughts.

One of his eyebrows arched very appealingly. "We could throw caution to the wind and go back for the day," he suggested.

"Do you like to live dangerously?"

He shrugged and that same brow went up even higher as he looked her over with an assessing eye. "You could go in disguise."

"In disguise?"

"A hat, maybe some sunglasses—"

"Sunglasses on a cloudy day?" she said dubiously.

"A rainy Sunday will draw all kinds. And I doubt if there'll be many reporters scoping out the window-shoppers looking for you."

"True." Blythe thought about it. More precisely, she thought about not leaving the house today, about what it would be like to spend the day marinating in temptation. That was dangerous when the previous night's unsatisfied desires were close enough to the surface for her not to be able to get her eyes off his rear end, even when she tried. "I'm willing to go incognito and chance being recognized, if you are."

"You're sure?"

Even in looser jeans his thighs teased the fabric, the wideness of his shoulders seemed somehow accentuated by that yellow shirt, his clean-shaven face with its square jaw and high cheekbones made her heart beat in double time, and her hands itched to run through that thick shock of golden hair. "Positive," she said with a vengeance.

Half an hour later they were on their way. Lee had raided the master bedroom and come out with a tweed sport coat that Blythe put on over her jeans, cuffing the sleeves and pulling both its collar and that of her red polo shirt up around her neck. The brown fedora she wore over her tied-back hair had been part of a Halloween costume, Lee had explained, and although it was something Blythe wouldn't have ordinarily worn, she felt very voguish. Since the hat sat barely above her eyebrows and cast a shadow over the rest of her face, she convinced Lee to forego the men's sunglasses he'd procured for her.

"One rule," he said as he came around and opened her door in the downtown Denver parking lot. "Today we're just two people out for a lark. No talk about the past or work or your formula or anything."

He held out his hand to her and Blythe took it. "Deal," she agreed.

They had brunch at the Westin Hotel, after which they crossed the connecting corridor to the upscale shops of the Tabor Center; they came out next to a store that sold framed prints. Blythe stopped to admire a large copy of a bright red poppy and from behind her Lee bent close to her ear and said, "I'm sorry, darling, but I can't live with that in our bedroom."

Blythe laughed and played along. "I suppose you like the line drawing of the old cowboy on the swaybacked horse better, dear."

"No, honey, I actually like the snow scene."

"To make your stuffed moose head feel at home?"

"Of course."

From there they went past a pet store with a variety of puppies in one window and kittens in the other. Lee draped an arm across Blythe's shoulders and leaned so close his cheek grazed hers. "No cats, honey bunch, you know I'm allergic."

"Me, too, sweet cheeks. Besides, we can't have Maude and Hershel nervous."

"On second thought..."

Blythe poked him in the ribs and moved to the puppy window.

"The Dobermans," he decreed. "We need some good watchdogs."

Blythe shook her head. "But, sweetheart," she cooed, "the schnauzer is so cute."

"One of each then. A Doberman for me, a schnauzer for you."

"And what about the kids?"

"You want a separate dog for each of the six of them?"

"Six children?" an older woman also admiring the puppies asked, obviously having eavesdropped.

Lee tightened his arm around Blythe's neck and pulled her in for a hug. "With number seven on the way," he confided to the gray-haired granny with a wink that made the older lady laugh.

"Congratulations," she said.

Lee thanked her, every bit the proud papa. Then, his arm still around Blythe's shoulders, he eased them back into the mainstream of shoppers.

"You're a wicked man," she teased him in little more than a whisper.

"You love it."

"Mmm," she admitted. And maybe him, too.

They lingered in the video store, where an old silent movie played on a miniature theater screen, and argued the merits of romantic comedies over Westerns. In the train shop whose facade was actually the end of an old Pullman car, they discussed buying their imaginary kids the most expensive set in the place. The high-tech gadget store kept their interest for over an hour as they tried out the sound-effects chair, dodged the salesman who took too seriously their discussion of how no home should be without the neon jukebox, tested the cooling capabilities of the fans in the safari hats, and played with the laser ball whose colored beams followed the movement of Lee's palm passing over it.

They bought jelly beans and cherry chocolates in the candy store, croissants in the French bakery, and Lee had a T-shirt made for her that said The Little Woman, for which he earned a punch in the arm and a mug from the next shop that claimed he was a stud muffin.

Through it all Blythe was very aware of his arm around her shoulders and of his hand taking hers. Because it felt so natural she found herself easily returning a squeeze of his fingers or using her free hand to clasp his bicep when she was making a particular point or standing on her toes to whisper something to him. It felt wonderful to be pulled against his side and she let him know by stretching her own arm across his back. And when he nuzzled her neck to camouflage a wicked comment about another couple she only eased the way for him, enjoying both the intimacy of sharing a private joke and the warmth of his breath against her skin.

They didn't leave the Tabor Center until it was closing for the day. From there they went to a grocery store to "stock the larder," as Lee put it, and buy the makings for their dinner—salmon filets and fresh artichokes.

It had stopped raining by the time they got home, but the sky was still heavily overcast and the air was too cold to seem like spring. Lee opened a bottle of wine for them to sip while Blythe whipped up a batch of chocolate cookies from a recipe she'd invented.

"I'm still not sure I want to eat something that has thorns," she told him, eyeing the pot on the stove where the artichokes steamed.

"I told you I cut the thorns off," he reminded her. "I can't believe a grown woman of the world hasn't ever eaten an artichoke."

"Grown I am. But who said I was a woman of the world?"

"Sorry, my mistake. I should have known only your dreams have taken you out of the research lab."

"And I have some doozies, too."

"*Doozies*," he repeated. "People don't really use that word, Coopersmith. Where'd you come from, anyway? The back of a turnip truck?"

"Doozies," she said again, as if beginning a recitation. "As in dreams where tall, black-cloaked figures impale me on the biggest, thickest post of Stonehenge."

He fought a laugh. "I'm going to say yes, you're right, that is a doozie of a dream—and try not to make any comment on the sexual symbolism of it."

Because her hands were coated with cookie dough she butted him with her hip.

"Don't you have any nice dreams?" he asked as if she'd scandalized him. "Like being whisked off to sun-drenched beaches to lounge in the sand while pygmies feed you artichokes leaf by leaf?"

"So your skin can burn and turn precancerous and you only have cacti for vegetables? Some dream. I'll stick with Stonehenge, thanks, just the same." She rinsed her hands and took a cookie sheet to the oven. "What do you dream about that's so great, Stud Muffin?"

He butted her this time. "Good things. Like being surrounded by a bevy of bikini-clad beauties."

"Nope, nothing sexual in that. And how come you get a bevy of bikini-clad beauties and all I get are pygmies?"

He winked at her. "I'm no dummy. This stud muffin doesn't want any competition."

They poached the salmon, made a lemon-butter-tarragon sauce for the artichokes, and baked two more sheets of cookies, drinking wine and teasing each other the whole time.

Just as they sat down at the dining-room table to eat, the electricity went out.

"What terrific timing." Lee's lascivious tone came through the darkness that enveloped the whole house.

"I beg your pardon. Now the last sheet of cookies won't bake."

"Aww, and all you have is three dozen of them. How will you ever survive?"

"It'll be tough. Good thing I have cherry chocolates as a backup." Her eyes had adjusted to the dark and she still could hardly see a thing. "Do you know if there are candles around this place, or shall we just eat by match light?"

"Sit tight."

Blythe heard Lee make his way back into the kitchen. He must have gone straight to the candles, because within moments he was back with three of them.

"Nothing fancy, but they'll let us see what we're doing," he said as he set the plain ceramic holders in the center of the table. "Not to mention that I couldn't have asked for a better mood setter."

Blythe agreed but kept it to herself. Instead she inquired, "It takes a certain mood to eat cacti?"

He sat down just around the corner from her and pulled the artichokes between them. "Absolutely."

"Does that mean if the lights had stayed on I wouldn't have had to eat them?"

"Now watch out—the little woman is never supposed to give her man a hard time." He pulled off a leaf and dipped the wide end into the sauce. "Here's how to eat it—you just sort of scrape off the meaty part at the bottom with your teeth." He demonstrated, pulled off another leaf, dipped it and held it up to her mouth.

Blythe looked at the leaf, then at Lee. "Funny, you don't look like a pygmy," she joked. Making a dreadful face she held his wrist and bit the end of the leaf, finding the outside rubbery while the inner side slid into her mouth like butter. When she'd swallowed it she said, "All I taste is sauce. Which is good," she added in a hurry, so as not to insult him.

"Okay. Try one without the sauce, then."

"I should have kept quiet," she muttered.

He held up another leaf for her and Blythe wondered if he was going to hand-feed her the whole globe. Not that she minded. "It's very mild. Sort of nutty tasting," she said after she'd eaten that one.

"Do you like it?" He sounded so hopeful she could hardly say she wasn't really sure, so instead she said, "Better with the sauce than without."

Lee pushed her artichoke closer to her dish and took a few leaves off his own. "It'll grow on you," he said as he squeezed lemon over his salmon.

Blythe did the same, disappointed that the lesson was over. "So you fantasize about bevies of bikini-clad beauties, huh?" she said into the silence.

"That was actually a pretty dated dream," he admitted when he'd finished a bite of fish. "It started during one of those awkward-kid stages."

He was too confident and comfortable with himself for her to imagine him as an awkward kid. "You must have been very young."

"I did some pretty dumb pranks to impress the girls in my sixth-grade class."

"Like what?"

"The usual demonstrations of affection. Stuffing snow down their backs, shooting spit wads at them, all those sophisticated things surging pubescent testosterone

causes." He ate some of his artichoke, obviously enjoying it. Then he asked, "What about you? Didn't you ever
do anything silly to impress a boy?"

"I'll never tell."

"Chicken," he goaded her.

"Through and through," she agreed, letting her eyes
feast on the shine of his thick blond hair and the angular
planes of his face, all gilded in the candle glow.

"Okay, then. If you won't confess to that, how about
one thing in your life you'd like to be able to do over
again?" he suggested.

"From childhood? All of second grade," she said after a sip of wine. "It was nine months of one embarrassment after another. I started off on the wrong foot. I'd
spent the whole summer in a gripping fantasy that I was
a particular movie star. I went in the first day and asked
the teacher not to call me by my own name—"

"Let me guess. You wanted to be called Shirley Tem-
ple."

Blythe shook her head. "I shouldn't tell you this, either."

"Sandra Dee?"

Another shake of the head.

"Hayley Mills?"

"Nope. Greta Garbo. And I was doing a bad imita-
tion of the accent at the time, too, which only made
things worse. The teacher burst out laughing and then so
did the rest of the class and I was mortified. There were
a couple of mean boys who called me Greta Garbo all the
way through high school."

Lee fought a smile. "They must have had crushes on
you."

"I don't think so," she said dubiously. After a bite of
salmon she went on. "Then some boy whose name I can't

even remember now kept chasing me at recess, tackling me and kissing me—big wet ones right on the mouth.''

"Ooh, my favorite kind."

"Oh, sure. Anyway, I finally told the teacher, but there was something about the way I said it that started her laughing again and I got to be the butt of that joke, too. Serious humiliation. Then I got caught talking while we were making sock puppets in art and had to stand in the corner. I was miserable.''

"Tough year," he commiserated. "I only have one question.''

Whatever it was, he could hardly keep a straight face asking it. Blythe waited.

"Did you make the sock puppet talk like Greta Garbo?"

She threw her napkin at him. "No, I didn't," she said, feigning indignation, even though she failed to keep herself from laughing. When she'd finished her salmon she asked, "What about you, wise guy? What one thing do you regret?"

He pushed his empty plate away, too. "Not meeting you a long time ago," he said without hesitating.

That pleased and embarrassed her at once, so Blythe joked about it. "Oh, yes. You've definitely come a long way from snowballs and spit wads.''

She reached for both of their plates to clear the table, but Lee stopped her with a hand on her wrist. "They'll wait until tomorrow morning.''

Blythe looked at him and could have sworn sparks actually flew from his eyes to hers. "Okay," she agreed, leaving the dishes where they were. But Lee didn't take his hand away. Instead he rubbed the sensitive inside of her wrist with his thumb in feathery strokes.

"So how would you have done second grade over?" he asked in a voice that was suddenly deeper, more sensuous.

"I'd keep a low profile—something I made sure to do forever after that," she answered, surprised to hear the timbre of her own voice sound very similar to his.

"And did you always avoid big wet kisses on the mouth?"

"Well, not always," she said coyly, wondering where the flirtatiousness had come from.

He smiled a very sexy smile. "Does that mean you learned to like them?"

"I guess it depends on how big and how wet." She was playing with fire and knew it, but somehow it didn't matter. What she felt for Lee was happening on its own, just the way the relationship had, and it suddenly seemed futile not to roll with this, too.

"How big and how wet do you like them?" he asked, insinuation thickening his voice.

"Pretty big and not too wet."

"Let's see if I can get it right," he said as he leaned over and kissed her lightly.

"Not bad," she said when he moved away.

"But not good?"

"I wouldn't say that."

"But it could be improved. With practice," he said in that smoky tone from the night before.

"Mmm," she agreed, all the while telling herself that if she didn't want this to go any further, she should stop it now, before it had really gotten started. But the truth was that she did want it to go further. She wanted it to go all the way. "You know what they say—practice makes perfect."

"I can't think of anything I'd rather do," he said wryly.

Blythe let her gaze follow the slight fan of lines at the corners of those aquamarine eyes to the creases on either side of his perfect mouth. "Me neither," she answered, only managing a breathy whisper.

"I've gone a little crazy over you," he told her then.

"I've gone a little crazy over you, too," she admitted. Not only was it true, but she didn't see any reason to deny it.

Lee's answering smile was a slow, lazy thing. "And there's nothing else in the world I want to do more than make love to you."

The sparks were not only going off between their gazes but from the spot he caressed at her wrist, too, shooting up her arm and igniting other embers that had been smoldering just under the surface since the night before. "You don't think it's too soon?" she asked, remembering that it was his agreement with that very excuse twenty-four hours ago that had kept her denying what her body had craved to the point of distraction.

Lee shook his head. "It can't be soon enough."

She kept staring into his face, so strong, so masculine, so fine. She cared about this man. More than she had cared about anyone in a long time. Maybe more than she had ever cared about anyone. Now there was a way of expressing it, an outlet for it. Nothing else mattered.

"I want you," he said.

She nodded, slowly, definitively, as if it were a foregone conclusion. "I want you, too."

Lee's hand slipped over hers and he stood up. Taking just one of the candles with him he led her upstairs and down the hall to the master bedroom. Blythe hadn't paid much attention to that room and still didn't notice more than the general cream coloring and the downy quilt that draped a king-size bed.

Lee took her all the way to the side of the bed, set the candle on a night table and turned to her. "Welcome home, sweetheart," he said, half-serious and half-teasing, the way they had been all afternoon.

Blythe smiled, but this time it was shaky as nerves caught up with her and she knew a strong fear of disappointing him. Why weren't her legs longer? Her waist tinier? Her breasts bigger? Why wasn't she more experienced?

"Relax," he said as if he were privy to her thoughts. He lifted first one of her hands, then the other, kissing the backs of all ten of her fingers in turn.

Amazingly enough, as Blythe watched him, as she felt the tenderness of his touch, the sweetness of his kisses, she did relax. In fact, she even started to think her tension of moments before was silly. This was Lee, after all.

She slid the hand he'd finished with up his arm and underneath his sleeve to the mound of his bicep, squeezing, massaging, letting herself remember that this part of him, at least, was familiar to her.

He placed the hand he still held to the side of his face, turning into it to kiss her palm and dampen a circle there with his tongue. It made her laugh softly, even as goose bumps skittered up her arm in response.

Then, leaving her hand to stay along his strong jawline, Lee reached around to the scarf that fastened her hair at her nape and untied it, dropping it somewhere behind her before plunging his fingers through her curls to cup the back of her head. He brought her mouth close enough to take it with his own when he closed his eyes and leaned toward her.

How could something be so satisfying and so electrifying at the same time? But that first press of his mouth over hers was. His lips were parted and warm, then opened wider. Blythe didn't mind. It wasn't as if she didn't yearn for as much of him as she could have.

His tongue thrust into her mouth and drew out again, in and out, a preview of things to come, and each time Blythe met it with her own, inviting it to stay awhile. Then his hand went up the back of her shirt and released a shiver of delight at that first touch of bare skin. Taking his lead, she slipped her hand out of his sleeve and pulled his shirt free of his jeans to do the same to him, reveling in the silky texture of taut flesh over bone and muscle.

All on its own her mouth opened wider still beneath his and Lee seemed only too willing to deepen their kiss into something else, something far more intimate and demanding.

His other hand went under her shirt, too, so he could slide both of them above her shoulders. He abandoned her mouth for only the split second it took to pull the red knit over her head and throw it away fiercely, as if he never wanted to see it again. Or maybe it only seemed that way because Blythe wanted so badly to be rid of his.

Her bra went next, but she was hardly aware of it as she unbuttoned his shirtfront and slid her hands up and over the wide expanse of his shoulders until he released her for long enough to let it fall to the floor behind them.

Then, with a groan that echoed in his throat as he plundered her mouth, a groan that sounded like need for release, he unsnapped the waistband of his jeans before wrapping his arms around her again.

Oh, how Blythe wanted to see, to feel, what he'd loosed down there! But she wasn't that uninhibited. Yet.

So instead she pressed a hard path with her palms up his
pectorals and around to his broad back, holding him just
tightly enough for her nipples to barely brush his chest.

Another groan came from Lee as he insinuated his
hands between their bodies and took hold of both of her
breasts kneading, squeezing, caressing with just the right
pressure, just the right rhythm to make Blythe groan this
time.

Then he was gone.

He let go of her, tore back the quilt and sheets on the
bed and turned to her again. "Come here," he ordered
in a raspy voice, grasping the front of her jeans to pull her
closer. He popped the snap and bracketed her waist with
both hands, sliding them down her hips and taking
everything she wore from there down with them, until
Blythe was naked in the golden glow of the candlelight.

"You, too," she urged, slipping her hands inside the
back of his jeans, just far enough for her fingertips to
reach the tightness of his derriere and let him know she
wanted him as free as she was.

"You aren't going to do the honors?" he asked with a
husky laugh.

But all Blythe could manage was a bit of a moan that
admitted her timidity on that count. He didn't push it.
Instead he unceremoniously dropped his pants and
kicked them out of the way. That was when he pulled her
up close against him and she got her first feel of the part
that had been straining his jeans before. Hot, hard and
satiny, that long, thick ridge made a place for itself
against the softness of her stomach.

Held tight to Lee, Blythe fell with him onto the bed. He
rolled her onto her back and rose above her just enough
to capture her mouth with his again at the same moment
that he found her breast with his hand. Oh, how he toyed

with her. One moment his touch was light, torturously scant, the next he traced just the outer shadow of her nipple with a single finger, before drawing only his thumb up and over the ultrasensitive crest. He gently pinched and rolled that hardened nub, then fitted it to the very center of his flattened palm to make lazy circles against it.

He drove her wild with wanting more and more and, just as she came near to asking, his mouth left hers and found its way there to appease her. Sucking, nipping, flicking with his tongue, until there was nothing left in her but a driving, aching need.

That was when he raised his thigh between hers. Slowly. So slowly. And then he was there, the corded length of that leg pressed against her, rocking against her, building desire as his hand burned a trail down her stomach and curved over and into the space his thigh had readied for it. Blythe couldn't keep her back from arching as he slipped a long finger inside her.

His mouth left her breast and once more his lips found hers, open wide now in the agony of anticipation. He rose over her, slid his hand back up her stomach and replaced it with the long, hard shaft of his desire.

Her body took him, all of him, willingly, welcoming him by closing around him and arching her hips up into his to take the full length and make him groan with the same divine agony he'd let loose in her.

He began to move. In and out, pushing so deeply into her that he touched a core she'd never known was there before and setting off white-hot explosions of glorious ecstasy that she never wanted to come down from. In the middle of it she felt him explode, too, his body tensing into one taut cord of steel over her, inside her, deeper still, until little by little the tide of pleasure began to sub-side and finally ebbed away.

Lee pushed himself up on his elbows and kissed her, a deep, bonding kiss. Then, holding her tight enough to keep them joined, he rolled them to their sides. The wonderful heaviness of one of his legs over her hip pressed her into the softness of the mattress. He let go of her long enough to pull the quilt over them, then put his arm back around her.

"Don't go anywhere," he said in a thick voice, set-tling his chin on the top of her head.

The sound of his passion-ragged voice, the feel of his warm skin against hers, the sensuous, earthy scents of their two perfectly mingling bodies, and the salty taste of that last kiss that had coupled them almost more than the act that had gone before—everything went with Blythe as she drifted into blissful darkness.

All the while knowing without any doubt that she loved this man.

Chapter Nine

The smoke detector went off at six the next morning. Jolted awake, Blythe wasn't at first sure where she was or what the commotion meant, but Lee shot out of bed and out of the room. A few minutes later the noise stopped and by then Blythe had realized what was happening. She'd gotten out of bed and put on the first thing she could find to run out of the house in—Lee's shirt.

Just as she finished her race to button it he walked back into the room. "It's okay. The power just came on again about an hour ago. We forgot to turn the oven off or take out that last pan of cookies, so they burned."

"But there's no fire?"

"Only a lot of smoke. I opened all the windows downstairs."

Knowing now that there wasn't any imminent danger, the fact that he stood there unashamedly naked finally struck Blythe.

"Get back in bed," he said. "It's still cold and rainy, and with everything open this house will be an icebox in a few minutes."

Lord, but he had a gorgeous body, Blythe thought as she looked at him. He was long and lean and taut and sinewy. The instant memory of the night before came to mind and what that body had felt like wrapped around her, against her, on top of her, inside her.

Blythe dragged her eyes up the line of sandy-colored hair that ran from his navel to fan out over his perfect pectorals and scatter toward his throat. By the time she got to his face he'd caught her staring.

His grin was lazy. "You don't have to just look. You're more than welcome to touch," he told her, issuing the invitation without a trace of arrogance as he got back into bed and held up the quilt for her.

Blythe put one knee onto the mattress but his "Uh-uh. No clothes allowed," stopped her.

Looking was one thing. Showing was something else. "I'm cold," she lied; the truth was that her temperature had skyrocketed along with her pulse rate in the past few seconds. She slid under the covers and found Lee just waiting to pull her over to him.

"Sure you are," he murmured with a laugh.

Without ceremony he unbuttoned the shirt and slipped it off, settling down with Blythe in his arms, her head on his shoulder.

"How are you this morning—besides shy?" he asked in a sensuously husky voice.

"Good," she answered, surprised by the near purr in her own tone. What was she—some kind of sex kitten? "How are you?"

He reached down a hand to her fanny and pulled her on top of him. "Let me show you."

The hard evidence was there at her middle, and desire sprang to life in Blythe as if it hadn't been satisfied the night before. Sex kitten? she thought again. More like sex maniac. And it was Lee's fault; she'd never felt such instant urgency with what's-his-name.

Lee arched his hips upward at the same moment as he took her head between both hands and brought her mouth to his. It was wide open, hot, and demanding enough to let her know that whatever had caused these quick flames in her had had the same effect on him.

His tongue ravaged her mouth with just enough roughness to feed the blaze burning inside her and Blythe met him thrust for thrust, parry for parry.

Maintaining his hold he rolled her onto her back and found her breasts with the same urgency. The ungentleness of his hands sent scattershot sparks into the conflagration and turned it into a wildfire that ran all through her. Wanting him the way she had the night before was nothing like what she felt now and she suddenly knew that she definitely wanted to touch.

Her hand was on the side of his waist and she slid it around to his derriere, testing its tautness with a grasp as firm as his on her breast. But that wasn't really the portion of him she was desperate to explore, so she ran her flattened palm down his hip to the tight muscles of his thigh, trailing her hand around to the inside and upward, so slowly upward that he tore his mouth away from hers and threw his head back as deep rumbles rolled from his throat. His grip on her breast tightened but grew still, and knowing that she had him in the same throes she was experiencing only heightened her own excitement.

She reached him, taking hold and reveling in both the feel of that thick shaft and the power her touch had. She explored its length, texture, the tip, tested pressures and speeds, firm and quick, soft and slow, then softer still, using only the bare brush of her fingertips until he groaned and rose beside her.

Then he was gone. Out of her hand, out of her arms, out of the bed. Before she knew what was happening he had her by the wrist and he was pulling her with him to the bathroom. There he turned on the shower and took her into the marble-walled enclave, closing the glass door after them. His mouth found hers again as he pressed her against the side.

Again she found him, this time with both hands, driving him quickly to a near frenzy as steam wafted around them and water sprayed their bodies, turning them slippery.

His lips and hands deserted her all at once to grasp her thighs and slide her up the wall until his mouth could reach her breast. Blythe wrapped her arms around his broad shoulders and her long legs around his hips, holding tight to keep that long, hard shaft against that part of her that cried for him to be inside. She pulsed against him and he flexed back against her as he tortured her nipple with his teeth and tongue, sucking, tugging, rolling until she thought she would explode.

And then he readjusted their positions and slipped inside her. Ecstasy burst in them both at once, making them cling hard to each other until passion turned back into sparks, fluttered and faded.

Blythe raised her head from the shower wall and let it fall onto Lee's shoulder. He turned his face into the side of her neck and kissed her softly. "I love you, Blythe," he said then in a voice that was barely a rasp.

"I love you, too," she whispered back, feeling she must sound as spent as she felt.

Gently he set her back on her feet and held her close for a while as the warm jets of water sprayed them. "I think I need a nap," he said with a weak laugh.

Blythe couldn't have found the energy to argue even if she'd wanted to.

He turned off the water and reached out of the shower for a bath sheet, wrapping it around them and using it to dry her off with strokes that threatened to arouse her all over again before he finished. Then he took her hand and led her back to bed.

In the soft cocoon of his arms, with the quilt around them, it occurred to Blythe that their relationship had taken two giant steps in the past few hours. Or maybe she should count each act separately and consider that they'd taken three giant steps—making love twice and professing their love for the first time. But none of it disturbed her. Instead she felt such peace and contentment that she curved into Lee's body as naturally as if she'd been doing it all her life.

And on the brink of sleep she forgot that she had a care in the world.

The telephone was on Lee's side of the bed, so when it rang and woke them up for the second time that morning, he answered it.

As he did so Blythe held the quilt to her breast and rolled onto her back to be able to see the clock on the night table at her side. She couldn't believe it was after eleven. One day was more than she should have taken from her work on the formula and here she was, lounging around in bed until nearly noon!

"It's for you," Lee announced a moment after he'd said hello, handing her the phone.

She cleared her throat, hoping her voice wouldn't sound as if she'd been asleep until just then. "Hello?"

"Don't tell me I woke you up," Gib answered.

Blythe grimaced and wondered if her brother realized just how close by Lee was. "There was a power outage up here. I guess the alarm didn't go off," she lied.

"Are you alone?"

Only if he didn't count Lee, who was silently kissing his way up her arm. "Sure, why?"

"I just got my mail," her brother said ominously.

"And you called to tell me?" she teased as she moved her head on the pillow and opened the way for Lee's rain of kisses to find her neck.

"Remember my telling you I'd had a message on my machine from somebody at the Executive Protection Agency? Well, apparently when the guy couldn't get ahold of me, he decided to write instead. I just got a note from him."

A little shiver ran across Blythe's skin, but she didn't think it had anything to do with what Lee was doing to her other earlobe. "What did it say?" she asked cautiously.

"How sorry the agency was that I decided against hiring the bodyguard they sent over, and that they hope I'll keep them in mind if I ever have need of any of their services in the future."

As the full implication of what her brother had just told her sunk in, Blythe stiffened. Lee must have felt it, because he reared back and cast her a questioning glance. She could only stare at him, but apparently something clued him in to the fact that this needed to be a private call. He mouthed the words, "I'll leave you alone," and rolled out of the other side of the bed.

"Did you hear what I said, Blythe?" Gib demanded.

"Yes, I did," she answered in a small voice, keeping her eyes on Lee as he looked for his jeans.

"I called their office the minute I read this note, and no one there has ever heard of anyone named Lee Farrell. Then I talked to the man they sent to your house and he claimed to have met me there that day. He said I told him you had refused his services. And then I gave him a substantial compensation for his trouble."

"Then who . . . ?" she started to ask.

"I don't know," Gib went on, sounding panicky. "But I think I should call the police."

"No!" Blythe said in a hurry, just as Lee took his jeans and left the room, closing the door behind him. Finally free to say more, she did so. "You can't do that, Gib. You know what a can of worms would be opened if the police got into this."

"A bigger can of worms than you being somewhere in the mountains with a guy who isn't who he claims to be? A guy we don't know from Adam?"

"You can't call the police." Now Blythe knew *her* tone was alarmed.

"Then at least give me the address up there so I can come and get you. And for God's sake try not to tip off your bogus bodyguard."

"Hang on," she said.

Her fingers were shaking as she picked up Lee's shirt, intending to wear it the way she had when they'd been roused by the smoke detector. Then it struck her that everything had changed. She didn't really know this man who owned the shirt and couldn't bring herself to put it on. Instead she pulled a sheet off the bed, wrapped it around her and went to the door. Only opening it a crack and holding on to it like a lifeline, she called, "Lee? What's the address here? Gib has some papers he has to bring me," hoping it sounded believable and worrying that he would balk at the idea. After all, she was really a captive and not a guest.

But Lee rattled off the address, obviously without having to look for it or even think about it, something that suddenly struck her as very suspicious.

"Thanks," she said when he'd finished, closing the door again. Back on the phone Blythe gave the address to her brother. "I can't believe this is happening," she said afterward.

"It goes from bad to worse," Gib agreed. "Can you lock yourself in somewhere until I get there?"

"I—" Her voice quavered and she stopped to calm it. "I don't know. There's a lock on the bathroom door but not anywhere else. How long will it take you to get here?"

"Half an hour or better. Maybe you should get out of there and go to a neighbor."

Not without the formula, she thought, but didn't want her brother to know she'd been dumb enough to let it get out of her sight. "I think I'll be okay here. Just don't drive too slow."

"I'm leaving right now."

Gib hung up, but with a million thoughts spinning through her mind it took Blythe a moment to realize he had. Then she put the phone onto the hook and sat on the edge of the bed.

If Lee wasn't the bodyguard, then who was he? And was he dangerous?

A moment later that thought struck her as ridiculous. Lee dangerous?

And yet, was anything she knew about him the truth? All she could really be sure of was that he wasn't who or what he said he was. Maybe everything had been a charade—his personality, his caring about her, his making love to her....

Blythe's heart was racing. She was light-headed. A cold, clammy perspiration dampened her skin.

But she knew she had to get a grip on herself. She pressed her hand to the beads of sweat on her upper lip and then rubbed her chin with a knuckle. The formula. That was the most important thing.

It seemed clear that Lee had to have something to do with EASY. There was no other reason why a stranger would insinuate himself into her life. And that put EASY in the greatest jeopardy. Along with the registered letter she'd let go of, too, she thought with a fresh wave of panic.

She had to get them back. No matter who Lee was, she had to get them back.

She stood up, fighting the vivid memory of what had happened on that mattress just hours earlier. Her hand was shaking as she opened the bedroom door and went down the hall to her own room. She changed into fresh clothes and combed her hair. Then she quickly packed her overnight bag with all the things she'd brought from home, wondering if she'd be able to get back up there to take it with her, or if she'd have to make some fast escape and leave it behind. She tried to force the muscles in her face to relax so as to appear normal and went downstairs.

"Everything okay?" Lee asked her as she crossed the living room. He was standing at the kitchen sink, rinsing the plates left from the night before and putting them into the dishwasher.

"Fine," she managed, a little too curtly, she realized. She stood on the dining-room side of the marble counter and for a moment couldn't do anything but stare at him.

This was Lee! a part of her shouted. Yet another part kept remembering that he wasn't who she'd thought he was.

She swallowed the lump in her throat and tried to smile. "Since you're almost finished with cleanup duty anyway, I really need to get to work," she said.

It was his turn to stare at her. Blythe watched that frown crease form between his brows. The smile lines around his eyes and on either side of his mouth smoothed out and disappeared. And then, in a very quiet, very somber voice he asked, "What did your brother have to say?"

She shrugged, hoping he didn't see the tremor she felt in the gesture. "He just wanted to check in. And, as I told you, he has some papers to bring me," she added, remembering her excuse.

But Lee kept looking at her, those piercing aquamarine eyes of his boring into her in a way that suddenly unnerved her. He shook his head and something in his expression told her that he'd seen through her.

"You know, don't you?" he said.

How could he look so familiar, rouse the same feelings in her that he had been inspiring since she'd met him, and even have a close enough bond with her to sense what was going on, yet not be who she thought he was? Not be the man who had protected her, comforted her, made her laugh? Not be the man she'd fallen in love with? "Do I know what?" she asked, afraid she sounded too innocent.

His lips turned into a thin line that wasn't quite a smile and he breathed a short, mirthless laugh. Then he turned off the water and left the sink to face her across the counter. "I don't know how your brother found out, but he just told you who I am, didn't he?"

"You're Lee Farrell—bodyguard," she said glibly.

"I'm Lee Farrell."

"But you're not a bodyguard?" she asked, as if it were news to her.

He shook his head.

"Then who are you?" And why was she still trying so hard to appear light and carefree, when he obviously knew it was a false front?

"I'm Lee Farrell Horvat—you've probably heard of me as Bucky."

That shocked her and for a moment Blythe just gaped at him. Then she asked, "Bucky the bridge builder?"

"That's me."

No wonder he'd reminded her of her former mentor and friend, Blythe reflected. Lee was the nephew Howard had raised. "I heard you were working in Seattle," she ventured.

"The job was finished. I got back a few days after you took the formula."

So there it was. The first time those words had been said. Suddenly she realized it wasn't kindness or compassion that had kept Lee from pushing her to talk about this before. No wonder his attitude toward her hadn't changed when he'd heard the accusations. He'd known all along what was going on. And he'd already passed judgment on her long before they'd even met. What she had thought was patience and understanding was only his mask set in place.

Quick tears flooded Blythe's eyes but she refused to let them fall. Instead she raised her chin and spun around, looking at the house as if for the first time. "And this place?" she asked in what she hoped was a cutting tone. "It doesn't belong to your friend, does it? I'll bet it's yours. That's why you knew your way around it so well, why you could even find candles in the dark.'' Her bottom lip started to quiver and Blythe bit it to make it stop.

"It's my house," he admitted. "And Chad doesn't own a bakery, he's my partner. He just borrowed the van from a place down the street from our office."

How could she know where the lies started and where they ended? She only nodded, still fighting for some control.

"How did your brother find out?" he wanted to know next, coming around to prop a hip on her side of the counter.

She adopted an angry tone to get the words out and keep the rest of her feelings inside. "The Executive Protection Agency sent him a letter saying they were sorry he couldn't use their services. He called and talked to the man you paid off. What we don't know is how you found out Gib was about to hire a bodyguard in the first place."

"Dumb luck," he told her.

As he recounted the events that had led up to his masquerade Blythe didn't say a word. She just stared, trying to see through him.

"I needed to get EASY back and playing bodyguard seemed like the best way," he finished.

That made her laugh, if the sound that came out could be called that, she reflected. "And I'll bet you've had the formula since Saturday when I was dumb enough to put it—and the registered letter—in your secret panel."

"They aren't there anymore, no," he admitted.

"You almost sound sorry."

"None of this has been easy for me."

She looked away.

"It hasn't, dammit," he said, speaking more loudly than before. "I went into this with a clear picture of you as the ungrateful villainess. I had one goal and that was to take EASY back. Period. But that clear picture has gotten more blurred by the day. I certainly didn't expect any feelings beyond anger for what you'd done to Howard to enter into it, but they have. I didn't worry about liking you and I sure as hell didn't plan to fall in love with you. And the more I've gotten to know you, the more I've learned about you, the more confused I've become. Why, Blythe? Why did you take the formula?''

"Where is it now?" she asked rather than answer him, staring out the sliding glass door at the rain.

"Nowhere you can get your hands on it."

"Have you given it back to your uncle?"

"Not yet," he said impatiently. "But it doesn't matter. You've seen the last of EASY and the registered letter. Just tell me why the hell you took the formula in the first place."

Blythe looked him straight in the eye. "I had to. I didn't have a choice."

"Why?" he shouted, throwing his hands into the air.

"Haven't you seen the changes in your uncle?"

"I've seen a big change in him since this started. But under the circumstances that's no surprise. He can't be expected to take it in his stride, the way he does most things."

"I guess that means you don't think what he has done—breaking into my house, coming in the middle of the night to scream from the front lawn—is too outrageous?"

Lee shrugged. "He's feeling desperate and unbelievably frustrated."

Blythe just shook her head. "You've been gone for most of the last year, so maybe you wouldn't have seen it," she said. "But what about your aunt? I can't believe she hasn't noticed the changes in Howard."

"She's noticed that he hasn't been himself since you started this."

"Howard hasn't been himself for over a year now."

Lee looked at her as if she'd gone crazy. "What's that supposed to mean?"

"It means that what you see as responses to what I've done is more than that. It means that your uncle isn't the same as he used to be—and it started long before I took EASY."

"Blythe—"

"A little over a year ago I started to see a change in your uncle," she explained quickly, cutting him off. "There were some lapses in memory and some strange behavior—small things that I attributed to overwork. He was putting in long hours on EASY, so forgetting where he'd put a file or being unusually short-tempered seemed to go with the territory."

"Of course it does."

"But then the forgetfulness got worse. Much worse. I knew he hadn't sent himself the registered letter for the idea for the formula and no matter how many times I encouraged him to do it, to take my experience as an example of the risk he was running, he just couldn't seem to keep the thought in his head. And every time I reminded him, not only didn't he have any recollection of my having said it before, but there was a time when he actually asked me why he should do something as silly as send himself a registered letter. At first I thought he was kidding—"

"Which of course he was."

"No, he wasn't."

"Blythe. . ." This time his tone was more patient than she could stand. "Over the years he's sent himself dozens of registered letters to protect his ideas."

"I know he has. But he honestly didn't remember why he should do it," she insisted. "At about the same time he also started to do completely irrational things—firing lab assistants at the drop of a hat over minor mistakes, refusing to trust a couple of the other chemists in the group and treating them so unreasonably that they left. Then he hired a girl fresh out of graduate studies without conferring with me or with Bob—the only other researcher left in the group by then. That wasn't like Howard, but not until we met her did Bob and I get upset over it. She was completely inexperienced, and since we were so shorthanded, none of the three of us could possibly give her the supervision and direction she needed. Bob and I went to your uncle and pointed that out to him. Howard flew off the handle and ranted and raved until Bob said he'd had enough of what had been going on and quit. About the time Bob walked out, Howard charged into his office and locked the door. I could see him sitting with his chair facing a wall, just staring at it. He spent two hours like that and when he came out he didn't remember any of what had happened. He wanted to know where Bob was and why *I*'d replaced him with that young girl, who he then railed at and fired on the spot."

"So he had a bad day. We all get in rotten moods occasionally, take it out on the wrong people and then would rather act like it never happened."

Feeling a measure of frustration herself, Blythe nearly shouted, "Two days later he came in and asked if Bob was on vacation!"

Lee held up his hands, palms outward. "My uncle may have been on top of things at work, but at home we got used to him being a little scatterbrained at times. If he was going through a rough patch with his work and he was preoccupied with it, he was likely to do and say about anything.''

''And not even remember when you reminded him of major events he'd participated in? Come on!'' Now it was Blythe's turn to sound dubious. She didn't wait for Lee to refute any more before going on. ''The day he asked if Bob was on vacation I knew there was more going on than overwork and fatigue could account for.''

''What about his work at the time? If he was so out of it, how was he making strides with EASY?'' Lee asked, taking a different tack to disprove what she was claiming.

''I don't know how he was doing it, but he was,'' she admitted. ''And every time I'd see proof of it, I'd be as tempted as you are to deny that anything was wrong. But when a man is three hours late coming to work because he got lost driving the six blocks from his house to the lab, or when he goes to the pop machine down the hall and ends up wandering around the lobby two floors below and can't find his way back, it's time to worry. I decided to do some reading.''

''Ah, Blythe—''

''And the more I read the more afraid I got that Howard has Alzheimer's disease!'' she exclaimed, blurting out her suspicion before Lee could go on.

He shook his head, obviously not taking her seriously. ''That is the most ridiculous thing I've ever heard.''

''I hope so,'' she said fiercely, once again aware that she was almost shouting. ''I hope to God that isn't what it is. I hope he has a chemical imbalance in the brain or something—anything—that can be corrected.''

Again Lee shook his head, as if to say there was nothing that *needed* to be corrected. ''I think I'm getting the picture. You thought Howard had something terribly wrong with him and for that reason decided you had to take EASY."

This time she did shout. "Would you listen to what I'm saying, instead of trying to find some misguided notion that led me to take the formula!" She forced herself to go on more calmly. "All I did was try to get him to see a doctor. But in spite of everything—including some disorganization that had started with the way he worked—EASY was still progressing and he said he couldn't take the time for a physical. Then he started to test the formula on the mice and rabbits. At first it was working like a charm—the weight was coming off the animals rapidly and steadily without causing any loss of energy or nutritional deficiencies or any side effects at all. But Howard insisted it needed some fine-tuning and he kept working with it.

"And then one morning I came in and found the mice he'd injected with EASY the night before had died. Howard swore he hadn't given them the formula and went right back to work. I hadn't actually seen him inject them, so I accepted it, but after that I made sure to watch whether he did or not. He went on *fine-tuning* the formula, and every time he'd inject the animals with it I'd come in the next morning and find they hadn't made it through the night. But Howard was totally irrational about it. He wouldn't accept that something he'd done to the formula had turned it toxic and there was no reasoning with him."

"My uncle has never been an unreasonable man," Lee maintained.

Blythe ignored his comment. "Then he called the manufacturer that was funding his research, the same company that had the option to license EASY. He told them he was ready for the pharmaceutical development investigator and the clinical investigator to join the project. I don't know how much you know about this process, but the development investigator comes in to decide what the best form is for the drug—pills, injections, so forth—and the clinical investigator sets up and oversees testing on humans. They're only brought in when there's been conclusive proof through successful animal testing that the drug is safe. There was no way they should have been called in on EASY."

Blythe paused to take a breath and slow the racing words. "I went in to talk to Howard about it, to have him cancel his request to have the investigators sent in before he embarrassed himself and ruined his reputation. But he went off on one of his tangents, swearing I was mistaken, that there was nothing wrong with EASY. He denied that any of the animals had died and pulled out those early reports on the successful testing as proof. I offered to work with him to see if together we could sort through what had happened between the time EASY was working and when it turned toxic, but he refused. The investigators were coming in, and to prove his claim that the drug was safe, he said he would take it himself. I couldn't believe it. But he was actually going to do it and I couldn't let that happen—"

"So you took the formula."

"I hoped he wasn't serious, but he filled a syringe with the stuff and was going to inject himself. I did some fancy footwork to talk him out of it right then, but that was when I knew I had to do something."

"So you took the formula," Lee repeated.

Blythe nodded. "When he finally left for the day I dumped all of the already mixed formula down the drain and then searched the lab to make sure I had every note, every scrap of anything to do with it and took it home with me. It wasn't until later that night that I decided the best repayment I could give Howard for taking me in five years ago was to reverse whatever he'd done to the formula, so that it was working again.''

Lee stared at her for a long, silent moment and Blythe had the impression that he was searching for a sign that would convince him she was telling the truth. Then he asked, "What about the registered letter?"

"It lists Howard as the originator of the idea," she answered flatly.

"And the call to Jackson Pharmaceuticals? You weren't negotiating with them to sell EASY?"

"I was talking to them about a grant for a new project of my own."

Silence stretched between them again. Lee's expression was sober but there wasn't anything condemning in it. "I knew there had to be a good reason for you taking EASY," he said after a time. "I just couldn't figure out what it was."

But he was so calm. Too calm, Blythe thought, for what she had just told him. "This isn't a figment of my imagination, Lee," she said, guessing that he didn't believe her.

"No, it's just your misinterpreting some things. You weren't involved with Howard's research on EASY. Maybe when he called in the investigators he had already put the formula back to the way it was when it was succeeding. Then the results from the failed tests didn't need to be logged—why alarm the investigators if he'd changed it back? It's like I said, he's always had a tendency to be a little absentminded at times, and as for the personality changes, well, I think your first explanation was right—overwork and fatigue and probably some stress thrown in as he realized what he'd actually come up with in EASY and then temporarily fouled it. If there was really anything wrong with Howard my aunt would have noticed something. *I* would have noticed something when I talked to him on the phone or came home to visit.''

Blythe wanted to shake him. ''Don't believe me, then,'' she challenged him. ''But whatever you do, don't put that formula back in Howard's hands. If he takes it, it could kill him.''

Lee paused a moment. ''Look, I believe you only took EASY because you thought you were doing what was best for Howard—''

''Dammit, stop patronizing me!'' she shouted, spinning around and starting to pace. ''I know you don't want to believe there's anything wrong with your uncle. I understand that. I denied it for a long time, too. It isn't anything anybody wants to face in someone they love, but what I'm telling you is the truth.''

''I know you think it's the truth.''

Blythe groaned and hit her forehead with the heel of her hand. Then she turned to face Lee, speaking more slowly and ennunciating each word carefully, as if that might have more impact on him. ''You can't give that formula back to Howard. If you don't believe another thing in the world, believe that to do that is dangerous. Nothing . . . *nothing* is worth the risk that he'll take it.''

''If I don't give it back to him, what do you suggest I do with it?''

''Give it to me and let me work on it.'' Those words changed his expression almost imperceptibly. But for the first time Blythe saw his trust in her innocence waver.

After a moment he asked, ''Why didn't you tell me all of this the night Howard came to your house? That was the perfect opportunity to defend yourself.''

"I took EASY to protect Howard," she said wearily, feeling as if she was between a rock and a hard place. "To protect him from himself and as an offshoot to protect his reputation and his dignity. To tell anyone, even you, would have been disloyal to him and put his reputation and his dignity in jeopardy."

Just then the phone rang. At first neither of them moved. Instead Lee kept staring at her as though he was trying to see if he really could believe her. It wasn't until the third ring that he went to answer it. After listening to what was being said on the other end he pinched the bridge of his nose and spoke into the receiver. "Yes, let him through." When he'd hung up he turned back to her. "Your brother is on his way."

She nodded. "He's coming to take me out of here."

That brought an instant frown. "You can't leave now."

"Are you going to give me back the formula?"

He didn't answer her right away and she saw his doubts more clearly.

She breathed a mirthless laugh. "No, you aren't going to do that. You can believe I *misinterpreted* what was going on with Howard, or you can believe I made this whole story up to cover my tracks because I really did steal EASY. But you can't believe I'm just plain telling you the truth and there's something wrong with your uncle." She shook her head. "Staying here with you isn't going to change any of that. You have to come to your own conclusions. Just do me one favor. Before you even consider giving the formula to your uncle, think about what I've said. Talk to your aunt. Talk to Howard. Get him to a doctor."

Blythe headed for the stairs and her room just as the doorbell rang. But Lee followed her rather than answering it. "I love you," he said from the bedroom doorway as she grabbed up the overnight bag she'd packed earlier.

It was on the tip of her tongue to ask how he could love someone he thought might be a liar and a thief, but she didn't. Instead, her suitcase in hand, Blythe went back to the door, ready to leave.

Lee stayed where he was, blocking her path. "Don't do this."

But finding out that he'd lied to her, tricked her, taking into consideration what he must have been thinking about her all this time, all these factors left her just wanting to put distance between them. Slowly she raised her eyes to his face, trying to ignore what felt like a clenched fist around her heart. "There are things you need to sort through by yourself. And there are things I need to sort through by myself," she said quietly.

His aquamarine eyes held hers for a long moment as the doorbell rang several more times in rapid succession. Blythe saw the muscle in Lee's jaw clench and unclench, then he slammed both of his hands against the doorjamb to heave himself away from it. He stood in the hallway and she had the sense that he was fighting the urge to bodily stop her from going.

Without looking at him again, that was just what she did.

Chapter Ten

It was still raining half an hour later when Gib pulled into the garage of his house on the campus of Hale Boys' Boarding School. Clouds hung heavy and gray like old goose down pillows, but Blythe was too miserable to enjoy the weather.

Gib had told her that he'd been by her house the day before and there were still a few reporters camped out front. That hadn't left her any choice; she'd had to agree to be his houseguest until the coast was clear.

Blythe sat at her brother's kitchen table while he made her tea as if she were a child home sick from school. Actually she was ill. Sick in spirit, sick at heart. And even the cozy touches of twin ceramic ducks in the center of the country-style table and the pale wildflower wallpaper Blythe had helped Gail hang didn't do anything to dispel the chill that emanated from somewhere deep inside.

"I don't have a lot of time before a meeting with the board," Gib said as he flipped up the bird-shaped whistle on the teapot and poured water into two mugs. "But I think we should talk about hiring a real bodyguard for you."

Blythe shook her head emphatically. "No way."

"This time we could go down to the agency, so we'd be sure the guy was who he said he was."

"No, not a chance. Not under any circumstances, Gib. Just forget it."

"But—"

"But nothing. I won't even consider it." She was sorry to be the cause of the deeply etched frown on her brother's face as he brought the mugs to the table and sat down, but nothing he could say would change her mind. There were few things in her life she'd ever been sorrier for than she was at that moment. Agreeing to have a bodyguard in the first place had been a big mistake.

Apparently Gib got the message because he dropped the subject and went on to something else. "One thing has been on my mind since this whole business with the formula started, but I didn't want to bring it up before."

And he wasn't too anxious to now, if the fact that he stared into his cup rather than looking at her was any indication. But the drive here had given Blythe the opportunity to tell her brother the whole story of who Lee was, how he'd come to play the role of bodyguard, and how he'd gotten the formula away from her, as well as what he thought of her reasons for taking it from Howard. She couldn't imagine what else Gib was curious about. "Go ahead, shoot," she said.

"*Are* you sure Howard has Alzheimer's and wasn't just under a lot of pressure because he knew he was working on the discovery of a lifetime?"

That made Blythe smile. It was like Gib to have hidden his doubts from her, rather than undermine her decision. "No, I'm not sure Howard has Alzheimer's. I'm not a doctor, after all. And, as I said, I hope he doesn't. But there is something wrong with him—of that I'm positive." Just as positive as she was that she had had no choice but to take the formula in the first place.

"There's not a doubt in your mind?" Gib asked.

"When there was a doubt I didn't do anything. And even after I was convinced there was something terribly wrong with him I agonized until I was blue in the face, trying to come up with how to help him. Taking the formula wasn't something I even considered until he threatened to use it on himself. And even then I didn't want to pull the rug out from under him and put him through what I have. Lord, when he lapses into his bad times he's confused enough without my adding to it by doing something he could only see as a betrayal. But he wouldn't listen to anything I said, he wouldn't even acknowledge that he'd fouled the formula, and when he started to threaten to take it himself just to prove me wrong, I had to do something."

"I wasn't criticizing," Gib said quickly. "It's just that I deal with kids all the time who do crazy things because they're under pressure or upset or frustrated, and with the formula going bad on him, Howard had all three conditions. Some people can behave pretty erratically under those influences."

"I realize that. But Howard was behaving erratically *before* EASY went bad, so it just isn't that simple. I wish it were."

Gib took a drink of his tea, again not meeting her eyes. "It surprises me that you trusted Lee enough to let him hide the formula. You never even showed it to me."

"Did you want to see it? I would have if I had known," she said, meaning it. She hadn't intentionally kept it out of his sight.

"No, I didn't want to see it. It just strikes me as strange that you let your guard down with him."

"And obviously I shouldn't have," she conceded. Blythe knew what her brother was fishing for, but to explain why she had trusted Lee meant she would have to account for her feelings for him and she didn't want to. In fact she didn't even want to admit to herself that she had any, especially not when he'd made such a fool out of her. "I was just stupid," she said under her breath.

"There was no way for you to know who he really was," Gib reassured her.

"And what do I do now? Just sit and worry about whether or not Lee gives Howard the formula? And if he does, if Howard uses it on himself to prove his point?" Blythe stared at the ceramic cow on the wall behind the table where she and Gib were sitting. "Maybe I shouldn't have left. Maybe I should have stayed with Lee and tried to force him not to give Howard EASY."

"How could you have done that? You tried to convince the guy, Blythe. If he's determined to give the formula back to his uncle, there isn't anything else you could have done to stop it." Gib paused a moment, as if weighing his next words. "Actually, as far as I can see there isn't anything for you to do now. You're out of it, after all. A member of Howard's family has the formula and the same information you did to decide whether or not he's mentally unfit. You can wash your hands of it." His words hung in the air a moment before he added, "Can't you?"

Gib had a point. "I should be able to, shouldn't I?" Blythe admitted.

"It certainly seems that way to me."

But it didn't feel that way to her.

Gib checked his watch. "I'd better head for my office. Gail will probably be home before I am tonight, but not by much. Will you be okay alone until then?"

Blythe managed a weak smile. "Sure. It isn't as if there's anything wrong with me," she said feebly.

"Well, get yourself settled into the guest room—"

"I still don't think it's a good idea for me to be on this campus. Howard is unpredictable and I'd hate for him to come looking for me here."

"I just remembered that Gail's sister is out of town for a training seminar. She won't be back for over a month. I wonder if it would be okay for you to stay in her apartment?"

"That would be great," Blythe said, trying to sound enthusiastic.

"We'll talk about it over dinner." Gib took his mug to the sink. "Maybe I'll take you girls out for a burger."

"Sounds good," she agreed reluctantly, the last thing she felt like doing was eating.

"I'll see you then," Gib said on his way out.

Even after her brother had gone Blythe didn't move from her spot at the table. Left alone in the silent house it wasn't the formula that was on her mind. It was Lee. And how thoroughly he'd duped her.

She'd felt so safe with him. Not just in the sense that he was supposed to be a bodyguard who would protect her from Howard, but emotionally safe. He was the first man since Jerry whom she had let get that close... had let herself fall in love with.

And all he'd had on his mind the whole time was tricking her into letting him get hold of EASY.

His actions wouldn't have been so hard to take if he hadn't toyed with her emotionally in the process. If he had just played bodyguard until she'd left some opening for him to take back the formula. But he hadn't done that.

How could he have started a personal relationship, knowing why he was really in her life? How could he have said and done things to draw her to him, knowing that as soon as he had EASY he was going to leave her in the dust? What had the personal side of this been—something to keep him from getting bored while he waited for his opportunity? Or had that been his plan—to woo her into doing just what she'd done, into trusting him enough to give him access to EASY?

The implications of that thought tightened her throat. Had his only interest in her been a means to the formula? Had he dangled romance in front of her nose, like a carrot to a donkey, in order to accomplish what he'd come for? And then, having accomplished it, why had he made love to her? Was that his payoff? His reward to himself for a job well-done? Or had it just been the ultimate coup de grace to pay her back for what she'd done to his uncle?

Ugly.

Everything that had been between them suddenly took on an ugly air. She felt so dirty. So used.

So stupid.

As stupid as she'd felt when she'd found out Jerry Nickles had done her out of her share of their joint research.

As Lee headed down the highway toward his aunt and uncle's house an hour after Blythe had left, he asked himself the same thing over and over again—how could she think Howard had Alzheimer's? Or any other serious illness, for that matter?

Surely, if she were right, Howard would exhibit concrete signs that Aggie would have seen and commented on. Signs that Lee or one of his cousins would have noticed.

But Aggie hadn't said a thing except how upset Howard was over what Blythe had done. And Lee had put in calls to all of his cousins before leaving home—not one of them had remembered anything too out of the ordinary in their phone conversations or few visits to Denver.

So what did that leave him with?

He didn't like the answer.

It left him with the likelihood that Blythe had just made up the whole story in order to convince him to give her EASY.

Yet he couldn't believe that, either.

"Great choices," he muttered. "Something horribly wrong with my uncle—or the woman I love as a lying research thief."

But saying aloud that Blythe was a lying research thief sounded ludicrous. After all, she had refused to accept credit for that earlier antibiotic discovery, even when he'd tried to force it on her, he reminded himself as he eased off the highway in Lakewood.

Besides, if she was guilty and trying to take over EASY, why hadn't she just answered Howard's accusations with declarations that the formula was really hers? Instead, she'd left those accusations unanswered; in fact she'd accepted them and demanded only that Howard be treated kindly and patiently.

"And what about that?" he asked himself. What about all the evidence he'd seen with his own eyes of how much she genuinely cared for Howard? Of how worried she was about him, even how much she regretted having put him through this? Those things hadn't just been an act.

No, he couldn't believe that Blythe had appropriated EASY for selfish or malicious reasons, then lied about her concern for Howard's health to get the formula back once she'd lost it.

So what the hell was he supposed to think? That stress and overwork had exhibited drastic signs at the lab that hadn't shown up at home or around the family?

That was possible, wasn't it? Maybe Howard relaxed enough at home for the erratic behavior and forgetfulness Blythe had seen not to manifest itself. And maybe, coupled with Blythe's misreading and overdramatizing what she was witnessing...

"An error in judgment," he said as he pulled up to the curb in front of Howard and Aggie's house. Blythe had just misinterpreted some bad moods and some harmless forgetfulness that his uncle hadn't shown at home. That was all.

"So why don't I believe that, either?"

Lee got out of the car. It didn't look as if his aunt and uncle were back from the cabin yet, but he opened the screen and tried the door, anyway. Finding it locked, he rang the bell, but when no one answered he found the key they kept on the top of the door frame and let himself in.

The curtains were all pulled and Lee went around opening them, letting in the dim light of the rain-soaked day. And as he did vivid memories sprang to life.

In the formal living room he had a flashback to so many years of putting up the Christmas tree. He could just see Aggie flitting around unwrapping ornaments, while he and his cousins all sang carols and argued over who got to put what on the tree. And sitting in the wing chair in the corner would be Howard, calmly untangling the worst knots of lights without so much as a cross word. "The patience of a saint," his aunt would say every year.

There were two windows in the family room, and as Lee pulled open their drapes the light fell on Howard's after-dinner pipe on the table beside the recliner. He remembered the running gag he and his cousins had played on Howard the week his uncle had turned forty. They'd taken turns moving that pipe to a different place every day and then, when Howard couldn't find it each night, they'd teased him unmercifully about going senile in his old age. Somehow the humor they'd always found in that little trick was lacking for Lee at that moment.

In the kitchen he raised the shade over the sink and the other one over the window in the enclave where the table was. There he had an image of his uncle calmly reminding each kid over breakfast not to forget lunch money, books, homework or baseball practice after school. He'd also been the one to remember the anniversary of Lee's parents' death every year, when no one else but Lee had.

And then, like a knife stab, Lee thought of the night he had had to confront Howard on Blythe's front lawn. What if his uncle's question about what Lee was doing there hadn't meant that Howard had assumed Lee would only be staying there during the daytime? What if Howard *hadn't* remembered that Lee was there at all?

"Ridiculous," he decreed aloud. That wasn't the Howard he remembered.

Just then Lee heard a car pull into the driveway and the garage door open. He shook off the doubt that had crept in like a shadow and opened the door that connected kitchen and garage.

"You see, Howard, that is too Lee's car out front. I told you so. I can't believe you didn't recognize it," Aggie said as they both got out.

But Howard didn't respond to his wife. Instead he winked at Lee. "Bucky! I hope you're here with good news."

Lee met his uncle at the trunk as the older man opened it, exposing two overnight bags, a box of food, another of cleaning products and a trash bag that seemed to be full of laundry. "I know how Aggie is every time you go to the cabin. She can't even spend one night there without hauling up enough groceries for a blizzard, scrubbing the place down and bringing back a load of washing. I just figured you could use help unloading the car," he said, not really sure why he'd dodged his uncle's comment.

Aggie went into the house as Lee took the suitcase Howard handed him, put it under his arm and transferred the second one to that same hand, so he could hoist a box onto his opposite hip. "So how were the mountains?"

"Great!" Howard exclaimed enthusiastically. "I didn't realize how much I needed to get away. I guess your aunt was right—I haven't rested a minute since I started work on EASY. But I'm a new man now." And to prove it he lifted the remaining box, gripped the laundry bag between his teeth and firmly slammed the trunk lid down. Then, taking the bag out of his mouth, he led the way into the house. "You didn't answer me when I asked if you were here with good news."

His uncle was sharp enough to catch that, Lee thought as he set the overnight cases on the floor and the box on the kitchen counter beside the one Howard had left there. "I just wanted to check in and see how you're doing," he said, realizing that his reluctance to say the formula was in his trunk meant that he needed his own belief in Howard's good health confirmed. No harm in that.

"Well, he's doing much better," Aggie answered as Howard wandered to the kitchen table and sat down in just the spot Lee had pictured him in before.

"Don't forget you promised me a cup of coffee, Ag," Howard reminded his wife, then said to Lee, "Believe it or not, Miss Organization didn't bring any up there with us."

"Will you have a cup, Lee?" his aunt asked.

"Sounds good." Lee sat down across from his uncle.

"So, have you found the formula?" Howard persisted.

Not only hadn't he forgotten about it, he wasn't easily diverted from it, either, Lee thought with satisfaction. But again he didn't answer his uncle's question. "Speaking of the formula—did you say you were finished with the animal testing of it?"

"Absolutely," Howard answered without hesitation.

"And it was successful?"

"You bet. I was all set to ask Healthco to send in the next crew."

"The pharmaceutical development investigator and the clinical investigator," Lee said, expanding his uncle's response.

"Right."

"You told me you had already made arrangements for those guys to begin the next steps."

"Of course he has," Aggie put in with a frown. "You told me you talked to them twice last week, Howard."

Howard just stared at Lee for a long while, his brow furrowed. Then he shook his head vigorously. "No, you both must have misunderstood. I'd finished the animal testing and was just about to contact Healthco when Blythe absconded with my work. But I haven't talked to the people there in months."

Aggie brought three cups of coffee to the table, passing them around before she sat down beside Howard without saying another word.

"What about the animal testing?" Lee pressed him. "Did any of them die?"

"Not a one. Blythe told you that, didn't she?" Howard said, rolling his eyes over his coffee cup as he took a drink. "She just made that up."

"Why?"

"Who knows why?" Aggie put in heatedly. "It probably had something to do with her plan to steal EASY for herself."

"Do you have any idea why she took it?" Lee asked his uncle.

"Greed," Aggie said before her husband could get a word out. "That formula is worth millions."

"I guess I was just wrong about her all along," Howard concurred. "You know I saved her rear end five years ago, when she tried to swipe another chemist's diet drink."

"And this is how she repaid him," Aggie added.

Howard narrowed his eyes at Lee. "What else did she tell you?"

Should he be honest? Lee wondered. But in the end he decided Howard had the right to defend himself. "She said your bouts of temper drove away all the other researchers working in the group and that you were forgetting some pretty important things."

Howard made a face that announced just how absurd he thought that was. "A few petty arguments, the flare of a couple of tempers, some personality clashes, forgetting a paper or a meeting—''

"Or to send yourself a registered letter to protect your idea," Lee put in. His uncle was obviously having no problem recalling what Blythe had referred to, even if he did have a different interpretation of it.

"So a few things slipped my mind," Howard finished.

"You know how he is, Lee," Aggie said defensively. "Especially when he's immersed in a project. He can remember every last detail about his chemicals and concoctions—''

"Except this time. This time, without a copy of EASY, he couldn't reproduce it."

"That was six years' worth of work," Howard said in a voice that was slightly raised.

Aggie went on as if neither of them had interrupted. "But when it comes to taking out the trash..."

"In forty-odd years he's never once remembered to do it without you telling him," Lee told her, finishing his aunt's ongoing complaint.

"That's right," Aggie confirmed.

And yet.

Why were those worry lines right between her eyes? Lee wondered. Those worry lines that everyone in the family knew meant something was bothering her. Something she wasn't talking about. Was it only the missing formula that caused them?

Watching his uncle, Lee continued. "Blythe also mentioned that you were considering injecting yourself with EASY to prove it was safe."

"Howard! You didn't?" Aggie exclaimed, obviously shocked by the idea. "You know better than to turn yourself into a guinea pig!''

"EASY was safe as mother's milk," he retorted. "And Blythe said it wasn't."

"But to take it yourself..." Aggie's voice faded.

Lee looked from his aunt back to Howard. "So how long has it been since you had a physical?" he asked, making it sound almost like a joke.

"Oh, yes, Blythe has definitely been talking," Howard said facetiously. "I think she wanted me to make an appointment, just to get me away from the lab long enough for her to take EASY and clean everything out, so I wouldn't have even a drop to work from. First chance she got, that's just what she did, too."

Aggie hadn't taken her eyes off her husband. "You didn't tell me she wanted you to see a doctor. What reason did she give?"

Howard waved a bony hand in the air. "Just what Lee said—that my temper was short and that I forgot a few things."

Lee watched his aunt watching his uncle, then turned back toward Howard. "How long *has* it been since you saw a doctor?"

"I'm healthy as a horse." Howard shot up from his chair and took his cup to the sink. "Now don't sit around here asking me dumb questions, Bucky. Go on back and get my formula away from her."

Lee glanced at his aunt, who still sat so quietly across from him at the table. "What do you think, Ag? Does Howard need a physical?"

A moment passed before she answered. "It couldn't hurt. You know he hasn't had his blood pressure checked in years. But there isn't anything wrong with him that some rest and relaxation and working less won't fix. He's right—he is healthy as a horse."

"Which brings us back to the subject at hand," Howard reminded them. "Are you any closer to getting EASY back?"

Lee told himself that he should go to the car and get the formula out of the trunk. Howard seemed fine, just the way he'd always been. Aggie seemed to have confirmed not only that Howard was healthy and there was nothing to worry about, but also that whatever changes there had been in Howard's behavior lately were from overwork and stress. Blythe must have just blown the signs of it out of proportion. Everything was all right.

Except for a few small discrepancies. And those lines between his aunt's eyes.

Aggie pushed herself to her feet and stared down at Lee. "You just bring EASY home and I'll take care of your uncle."

"How did you know where to find me?" Blythe asked, when she answered the knock on Gib's front door late that afternoon and found Lee standing on the porch.

"I drove by your house first and saw the reporters still hovering around. I figured your brother's house was the next most likely place you'd be, so I looked him up in the phone book—and here I am."

Blythe stood blocking the door, aware that her gaze was running all the way up the tall, powerful-looking body that had allowed him to pull off his masquerade. He was wearing jeans and a black turtleneck T-shirt underneath a black cloth bomber jacket. The darkness of his clothes set off his light coloring. The angular planes of his face were sharpened by the serious expression that molded them, but his golden hair was somehow untouched by the dampness that lingered in the air, even though the rain had stopped.

A part of her reacted instinctively to the sight. She wanted to reach out a hand and pull him inside, wanted to have him wrap those long arms around her and comfort her, make her feel all right about what was going on, the way he had until this morning. But a stronger part of her wouldn't let her forget that for the past week he'd been wooing her and thinking she was a research thief at the same time.

"What do you want?" she asked as if she were in total control when she was anything but.

"I need to talk to you. Can I come in?"

She was alone in the house and a ripple of something very like fear ran through her at that question. What was she afraid of? This man who had fooled her? Herself? She raised her chin. "Did you give Howard the formula?" she demanded, as if only the right answer would buy his entrance.

"No, I didn't," Lee told her, and it was clear by the lines those words etched in his face that he was troubled.

Blythe stepped out of the way, wondering why the knowledge that he hadn't yet turned EASY over to Howard shouldn't afford her more relief than it did.

She closed the door and leaned back against it, watching Lee walk into the center of the rust and brown living room before he turned to face her.

"After I saw the reporters still at your house I put a stop to the media's interest in you. Howard told me he'd gone through the phone book and called every newspaper, radio and TV station listed, so I did the same thing, identifying myself and telling them there had been a misunderstanding all the way around. They seemed to believe me. Apparently some of the things my uncle said in interviews led them to believe he was . . . confused."

"And did that convince you that I was telling you the truth?"

"No, it didn't. I convinced myself about it before I ever headed to your house."

Blythe ached for the pain she heard in that admission. It made her soften her tone. "Then you know there's something wrong with Howard?"

She saw him take a deep breath that raised his shoulders into a shrug. Then he threw up his hands. "I don't know." He spoke in a way that let her know he really did know, but just didn't want it to be the truth. "I went to see him after you left his morning. He and my aunt were just coming home from their cabin and he wasn't any different than I've ever known him to be—"

"He goes back and forth," Blythe interrupted. "There are times when he does seem perfectly normal. That's the loophole I'd use every time I'd start to have to face something being wrong with him. He'd have a good week or a good couple of days and I'd excuse what had happened during the bad ones. But the good times are getting less frequent and the bad are getting worse."

"I just don't know!" Lee reiterated in obvious frustration. He jammed his hand through his hair and spun around, pacing into the hallway and back again.

"Then why didn't you give him the formula?" she challenged.

He kept on pacing. "A lot of reasons. A look on my aunt's face. The fact that Howard had forgotten to send himself the registered letter protecting his idea. Thinking about how he wanted to rush over to your house when I first called and told him I was playing your bodyguard—how that didn't make sense and I'd felt as if I wasn't getting through to him. Remembering how unusually excitable he's been through this. How he showed

up on your front lawn like some kind of madman—'' Lee
tripped over that word and stopped short, as if uttering
it was something terrible.

"Damn," he breathed. Then he shook his head like a
dog shaking off a tick and went on. "I remembered how
hard it was for me to reason with him that night, how
he'd acted surprised to see me there. I thought about him
alerting the media, when he'd sworn he wanted your
having EASY kept quiet. About his mood, his whole attitude, changing from one minute to the next." Lee hit
the plaid rocker-recliner with his fist and set it spinning
and crazily swaying. "And I couldn't get it out of my
head that he sat there and told me he hadn't called
Healthco yet to have the investigators brought in, when
he'd specifically told me he had and my aunt confirmed
it." He lowered his voice. "I hope to God you're wrong
and there's an explanation other than Alzheimer's. But
what you're right about is that something is definitely
going on with him."

Blythe just nodded. She realized for the first time that
somewhere deep down she'd still been holding onto a
glimmer of hope that maybe if she was the only one seeing the signs in Howard, they weren't really happening or
could be attributed to something else. But with that last
tiny flicker gone a heavy sadness came over her and her
heart went out to Lee all over again. "I'm sorry," she
said softly, taking her eyes off him and staring at the still-
swaying chair to force herself not to go to him.

"I also didn't give him the formula because of you,"
Lee said in a tone that was suddenly deeper, more intimate.

Blythe fought so hard to keep herself pressed against
the door that there was nothing left to even answer him
with.

He went on anyway, in that same black-velvet voice. "I knew there couldn't be any other reason behind you taking EASY. Whether I wanted to admit it or not—and believe me, it's one of the hardest things I've ever done—that was what convinced me that something was wrong with my uncle."

He came to stand in front of her, taking the papers out of his jacket pocket and handing them to her. "I'm sure you were only doing what you said you were—trying to retrace his steps and put the formula back to where it was when it was working. I'd like it if you'd finish that."

His words, his tone, stroked her as surely as his hands had only the night before. But still Blythe pressed herself into the door, taking the papers and looking only at them. "What about Howard?"

"I didn't tell him I had EASY."

She nodded. "But what about his health? He needs to see a doctor to determine what actually is wrong with him. He needs medical attention—there are drugs that might help, even if it is Alzheimer's."

"One way or another I'll get him to doctor. Even if I have to roll him up in a rug and carry him. I'm also hoping that if you fix the formula and return it to him, it'll help convince my aunt, at least, that something else is going on, that you didn't just take EASY for personal gain. I think she's worried about him, but doesn't want to face the truth any more than I did."

"I can't believe that anything to do with me at this point is likely to carry much weight."

"It could help if you were her niece-in-law."

Blythe grew cold. Very cold.

"I love you," he said. "We're good together—no, better than good—perfect. The one thing I'm sure of in all of this is that we belong in each other's lives."

Yesterday she would have agreed. And even now a part of her cried out to.

But a stronger part wouldn't let her forget that things weren't what they'd seemed to be since she met him. A moment out of time. Suddenly that was very much what their days together seemed like. All of them. The reality was that she didn't really know this man. Until this morning she hadn't even known who he actually was. And even now all she knew without a doubt was that he was capable of going to great lengths to deceive her.

How could she base her future on that?

She couldn't.

Blythe shook her head, looking over her shoulder. "Hopefully Jackson Pharmaceuticals will give us the funding for the Alzheimer's drug research. I want to concentrate on that," she said, as if he'd only asked her what she planned to do from here on.

"Great. There's nobody in the world I'd rather have working on it. But that doesn't have anything to do with marrying me."

Her hands were shaking and she pushed them flat against the door behind her. "I can't marry you," she told him, hating the tremor in her voice.

"You love me, you told me so yourself."

She looked Lee in the eye. "I loved the person I thought you were."

He started to say something, but cut it short. He shook his head and let it drop forward for a moment, rubbing the back of his neck before looking at her again. "I can't deny that I lied to you about who I am. But there were extenuating circumstances, Blythe. I didn't do it to hurt you, I did it to help Howard."

"But you did it," she said, aware that wounded pride was putting strength into her voice.

He threw out his arms. "What you see, what you know about me is what I am. The *only* thing I lied to you about was being a bodyguard. Even my name was the truth—with just the omission of Horvat at the end."

"The truth is that I don't know very much about you at all. You weren't exactly open about anything."

"Blythe—"

"There's nothing else to say. You put a good joke over on me. I never saw through you—not for a second. But that isn't what I consider inducement to marry someone." She raised the papers she held in one hand. "I think it's better if I just finish what I started here and we forget all about this last week."

"You don't mean that."

"Yes, I do."

"What can I say—?"

"Nothing." She could feel his eyes on her as if they generated heat, but couldn't raise her own gaze to his face.

After a moment he said, "You know me better than you think you do."

But all Blythe could do was shake her head. Since she'd found out who he really was and why he'd come into her life, she'd had too strong a sense of not knowing him to believe that now. "I'll go right to work on EASY and get it back to you when I've fixed it," she said flatly.

"And that's all you have to say?"

She nodded.

For a moment he didn't move; it was as if he hoped she might change her mind. Then Blythe stepped away from the door, turning her back to him.

"Damn you," he said under his breath.

She heard the door open, heard him go out.

But even without that evidence she knew he was gone by the feeling of emptiness that had its starting point inside her.

Chapter Eleven

Lee was nursing a straight scotch and staring at the sunset when his doorbell rang early Thursday evening three weeks later. He wasn't expecting company, so his first hope was that the drop-in was Blythe—even though he had no reason to hope for that. They hadn't so much as spoken on the phone since he'd turned EASY over to her. But today of all days, his craving to talk to her, to see her, to just have her in the same room with him, was intense.

So was his disappointment when he opened the door—to Chad. "Hi," his friend said a little gruffly, clearly trying to hide the uneasiness Lee could see, anyway. "I took a chance that you were home."

"Come on in." Lee opened the screen and held it for the shorter man. "Want a drink?"

"Sure."

As they went into the living room Chad nervously loosened the bright, flowered tie he'd worn to work. "I...uh...couldn't wait until tomorrow to know what the doctor said about Howard, and I didn't want to hear the news over the phone," Chad explained, going to the wet bar to pour his own scotch. When he had done so he turned and faced Lee. "It wasn't good, was it?"

It had taken Lee a week to get past both his aunt and uncle's anger over the fact that he wasn't giving them back the formula, though he had told them it was in a safety deposit box, so there wouldn't be any more raids on Blythe's house. He'd used EASY as leverage to get them to agree to Howard seeing a doctor. The battery of tests had taken the second week, and Lee had left the office early this afternoon to drive Howard and Aggie to the doctor's office to finally hear the results. "Howard has Alzheimer's," Lee said flatly, following it up with a pull of scotch.

"Damn," Chad breathed, shaking his head, pursing his lips, staring at the floor.

"Yeah. Damn," Lee agreed.

"How did everybody take it?"

Lee shrugged. "Today wasn't one of Howard's better days, anyway. He just sat there and didn't say a word. I'm not sure it sank in. Aggie cried."

"How about you? How are you doing with it?"

Lee went back to the window he'd been staring out before, leaning a shoulder against the glass. "My aunt finally admitted on the way home that she's known something was wrong for more than a year now," Lee told his friend, rather than answering his question. "She was aware of the mood changes, the forgetfulness, the disorientation. But she hung on to the times when he seemed fine and convinced herself Howard just needed to slow down. And since she didn't think anyone else had noticed anything, she felt more sure that what she was seeing wasn't serious. The first time she realized she wasn't the only one who saw a change in Howard was when she found out Blythe had been trying to persuade him to see a doctor.''

"What happens now?" Chad asked.

"We left with a couple of prescriptions for him to take. Beyond that . . .''

"Will he be able to work at all?"

Lee shook his head. "He'll need to be at home, where my aunt can keep an eye on him. His threat to try EASY out on himself was proof that it's dangerous for him to be unsupervised or deal with chemicals that could hurt him.''

"Does that set them back financially?"

"They'll be okay. There's savings and he has disability insurance. If and when EASY gets on the market, they'll be in great shape, and if for some reason it doesn't, I'll make sure they have whatever they need.''

For a few minutes there was no sound but the ticking of a clock. Then Chad asked, "Are you doing all right?"

Lee turned and leaned back against the window. "As all right as I can be. It didn't come as a complete shock. The doctors have been subtly preparing us for this all week. Howard has his wife and family behind him, come what may.''

"Will your aunt be okay with all of this, do you think?" Chad asked tentatively.

"Today I got the medicine, took Howard and Aggie home, and went in with them to call my cousins. When I got off the phone I found my aunt in the kitchen, kneading the hell out of a lump of bread dough. She was back to the way I've always known her—in control, strong, determined that she was going to get both her and my uncle through this. I looked at her and I knew she'd do it, too. She'll pick herself up by the bootstraps and pull Howard along with her, she'll do it with dignity and always with what's best for him in mind, loving him all the way."

Lee finished his drink. "Then she shoved me out of the house and told me to take care of getting EASY patented for Howard—and to leave my uncle to her." He laughed. "It made me jealous as hell."

"Jealous?" Chad repeated, sounding confused.

"There's nothing good about Alzheimer's. But at least Howard won't go through it alone. I thought about that all the way home and then I came into this big, empty house...." He shrugged. "I guess I'm just feeling sorry for myself because the woman I love, the woman who loves me, isn't anywhere around."

"So why don't you do something about it?"

"I've tried. I've called so many times, I now have a close personal relationship with her answering machine. I've gone by her house every chance I've had and she won't come to the door. I may be a little dense, but I think she's trying to tell me something—like that she meant it when she said she didn't want me." Lee went to the wet bar, stood next to Chad and poured himself another splash of scotch. Then he held his glass up in a toast to his friend. "Count your blessings for finding a woman who'll have you."

They both drank to that. Then Chad waved off the refill Lee offered. "You know what they say—there are more fish in the sea, and the best one hasn't been caught yet."

"I won't tell Marcie you said that."

"She does have a friend she's been wanting to introduce you to...."

Lee made a face. "No, thanks." Then he glanced at his watch. "Didn't you tell me this morning that you had a dinner party to go to tonight?"

"It's not important."

"And you're a lousy liar. Go on and get out of here. I'm okay."

Chad looked at him as if judging for himself. "You sure?"

"I'm sure."

His friend nodded toward the bar. "Are you planning on diving into a bottle of scotch to get you over our lady biochemist?"

Lee laughed. "I don't think that would do much good. I just have to accept that she doesn't want any part of me." He led the way to the front door. "Hell, this is the week for accepting the unacceptable."

Blythe made the drive into downtown Denver late Friday afternoon with her radio blaring—the better to drown the sound of her own thoughts.

Three weeks of intensive work isolated in Gail's sister's apartment, where no one and nothing had disturbed her, had paid off—EASY was back to being a successful formula for healthy weight loss. And once she handed it over to Lee, she could move back into her own house and go on with her life.

She'd looked Lee up in the phone book and discovered that the office of Horvat and Ingalls, Inc. was in the same building under which she and Lee had met Chad and his borrowed bakery truck to elude the media. Parking in that underground garage now made Blythe's stomach jittery. Maybe she should have had Gib return EASY, she thought.

Then she reminded herself why she hadn't let her brother do this. In the first place Gib was a busy man, and she'd already taken up more of his time than she had a right to. In the second place she wanted to hear for herself how Howard was, whether or not Lee had taken him to a doctor, and if so, what the diagnosis was.

The fact that she had to see Lee to accomplish all of that was just something she would have to deal with. Not that she thought it would be too awful. She was sure she was in control of her feelings for him and knew her decision not to go on with the relationship—let alone marry him—had been the right one. Now if only she could get her stomach to quit jumping around!

She took a deep breath, rejected the urge to look into the rearview mirror to check her tied-back hair, absolutely refused to wish she had worn something more attractive than jeans and a camp shirt, and willed her stomach to calm down.

The entrance to the office of Horvat and Ingalls, Inc. on the twenty-second floor was a wall of glass with the company name stenciled in black block lettering. As she opened that door Blythe called herself a fool for the millionth time in the past three weeks. It was no wonder she'd thought Lee an unlikely bodyguard. This plushly carpeted office, the pretty young secretary, sitting behind a walnut desk stationed between two carved doors that were more than likely the private offices of Horvat and Ingalls, all of this was definitely a setting more fitting for Lee. Why hadn't she listened to her instincts?

"Do you have an appointment?" the secretary asked when Blythe told her she needed to see Lee.

"No, I don't, but I called earlier and you said he was going to be in the office all day. If you'll just tell him Blythe Coopersmith is here, I'm sure he'll see me."

The young woman picked up the phone, pushed a button and relayed the message. Then she set the receiver back on the cradle and pointed a manicured finger over her right shoulder. "You can go in."

Yes, she could, if only her knees hadn't turned to mush. "Thank you," Blythe said. It took a deep breath to put the starch back into her legs and get her to that door.

The interior office was huge. A long conference table took up one half of it, while a drafting table and an L-shaped desk shared the other half. The wall opposite to the door was windows floor to ceiling and it was there that Lee stood, only partially turned away from them, the desk between himself and where Blythe stopped in the center of the room.

He was dressed in a gray suit with a crisp white shirt. His tie was black, the pattern on it an aqua blue that brought out the color of his eyes. Standing there tall and straight, one hand in his pants pocket, the other at his side, he looked so perfect that a photographer could have posed him. One glance made Blythe's mouth go as dry as toast and it didn't help any that for a long moment he said not a word, simply staring at her, his expression as blank as if she were a stranger on a job interview.

"I'm finished with EASY," she said all of a sudden.

He nodded slowly, those eyes of his staying on her the whole time. "I assumed," he said in a tone she'd never heard from him before; it was impersonal, formal.

She opened her purse and took out the manila envelope into which she'd put both Howard's notes on the formula and her revised version, setting it on his desk, then taking a step back. "EASY is working again, Maude and Hershel are in great shape, and I tested it on a couple of rabbits, too. Everything is documented, but don't be surprised if Healthco wants to do some more extensive animal testing on their own before going on to the next stages."

Again Lee nodded while he kept right on staring at her. "I've talked it over with my aunt and we want you to take partial credit, as well as a percentage."

Blythe shook her head. "I don't want it. I did this to repay Howard."

"Maybe you don't realize what this is worth."

"I don't care," she heard herself retort involuntarily in her effort to keep suppressed what was coming alive in her. For three weeks she'd worked on EASY almost every waking hour, using it to keep herself from thinking about Lee or about Howard. She had convinced herself that what she'd managed all that time to escape was gone for good. This was a rotten time to find out she'd only been kidding herself. "How is Howard?" she managed, wanting to get Lee talking so she could reclaim her control, wishing he'd look somewhere else.

"You're a good diagnostician," he said, more quietly than he'd responded before.

Her eyes suddenly stung. "Oh, no."

"The test results just came in yesterday." The single fist at his side opened and closed in a grip tight enough to whiten his knuckles.

Blythe's first instinct was to rush to Lee, to comfort him, to go to him herself for comfort. But she knew that if she took one step nearer, she'd lose herself to the feelings she had for him, feelings she didn't want to have. "How is he taking it?" she asked.

Lee shrugged. "We can't really be sure. He's not saying much."

"What can I do?"

"Find a cure?" he suggested sardonically.

"It looks like Jackson Labs is going to come through with funding for me to do drug research," she informed him, ignoring his sarcasm. "I meant, what can I do for Howard?"

Lee nodded toward the formula on his desk. "You've already done a lot."

"Do you think he'd see me?"

"Give it a little while yet. I'll let him know what you did on EASY and that it's gone on the way he wanted it to. He needs some time to adjust to this bombshell. Maybe in a week or two...."

"Sure. I'll call your aunt." What more was there to say?

"Blythe..." Lee headed toward her and she nearly jumped back.

"No." She could tell by the sound of his voice, by the look on his face, that what he was about to say had nothing to do with his uncle; she also knew her resolve was too weak at that moment to withstand anything else. "I have to go," she told him, spinning around and rushing out the door.

She heard Lee call her name again as she nearly ran through the outer office, but didn't stop. Instead she made a fast dash into the open elevator, punched the lobby button and closed her eyes tight until the doors shut and she felt the jolt of descent.

It should have felt good to be home, but as Blythe unlocked her front door and went in for the first time in over three weeks, she felt anything but that. Grateful, maybe, not to have had a car accident driving home through rush-hour traffic in a full-blown, sobbing attack of misery, but not good.

Her phone rang just as she reached her bedroom with her suitcase. When she heard her brother's voice on the answering machine she picked it up and sat down on the bed. "I'm here," she said in a nasal tone that she knew announced her mood.

"How did it go?" Gib asked.

"Fine," she replied, going on to tell him about handing over EASY and what she'd found out about her old friend.

"And then you cried all the way home?" her brother guessed.

"Pretty much," she admitted, it was useless to deny it. "I really was hoping I was wrong about the Alzheimer's."

"But we both know that's not the main reason you're bawling like a baby."

"Shows how much you know," she said around hiccups.

"I know if you feel this bad you must really love this Bucky the Bridge Builder."

"A person can't love someone they don't know."

"Ever hear the saying, 'You never know somebody until you live with them'? We all fall in love with strangers in one way or another."

"I did live with him and he was still a stranger."

"Are you sure?"

"What do you mean, am I sure?" she asked peevishly. "Of course I'm sure." Her nose was running, she couldn't reach the tissues on the other nightstand, and didn't feel like sparring with her brother the way he apparently wanted her to. "I can't talk now, I'm a mess," she groused. "I'll call you later."

As she hung up she noticed the light on her answering machine that flashed for the number of calls recorded since she'd been gone. She hit the button to play them, then fell across the bed and dragged the tissue box to her stomach as she listened.

There were a few reporters from various news stations and papers asking for interviews or her comments about Howard's accusations. Then Lee's voice came on.

She groaned a lament and pulled a pillow over her head. "Leave me alone!"

But the messages kept coming.

He apologized, but didn't plead. He said he thought they had enough going for them to get past this. He kept her updated on what he was doing with Howard. He asked how her work on EASY was coming. He missed her. He loved her. He believed she loved him. He wanted her to marry him. Why couldn't she see that what he'd done was for Howard, just the way her taking the formula was for his uncle's sake? Then there were a lot of hang-ups. One "Fine, dammit, if you don't want to be reasonable, forget it." Then another apology for losing his temper and a simple statement. He was accepting that she didn't want anything to do with him and wouldn't bother her anymore.

After that there was a click and three soft beeps to signal the end of the messages. The room seemed suddenly much emptier than it had as Lee's deep, rich voice had boomed into the space.

Blythe wrapped her arms around the tissue box, hugging it tight, and rolled onto her side as a fresh wave of tears flooded. She pulled up her knees, tucked her chin into her chest and cried until she was exhausted, all the while desperately wishing she still had work to drown herself in, the way she had these past three weeks, to keep herself from facing what she was feeling now.

Finally she fell asleep.

When Blythe woke up the only light in the room was the neon blue of the numbers on her alarm clock. It was after midnight and her face was stiff with the salt of dried tears.

Feeling like something a cat wouldn't bother to drag in, she got out of bed and went into the bathroom. The light blinded her and when her eyes finally adjusted to it the first thing she saw was her own reflection in the mirror.

She groaned at the puffy-faced, matted-haired mess that stared back at her. The cat wouldn't drag her in; one look at her and the poor thing would die of fright.

She turned to the linen closet for towels and a washcloth, opened the door—and came nose to leather with Lee's Dopp Kit.

He'd packed his things after she'd cleared hers out of the bathroom in preparation for their mad escape from the media. Apparently he'd forgotten the shaving gear. And of course he hadn't missed it, because the secret hideout they'd gone to had really been his own house, where he'd no doubt had a replacement.

Not that she had so much as guessed that the house was his until she'd found out who he was. She should have, though, she thought now, realizing that the house—like his office—suited him. Clean lines, casual elegance, understated good taste....

Her brother's words from hours earlier suddenly came back to haunt her—was Lee such a stranger to her, she asked herself, if she knew him well enough to realize what kind of surroundings he fitted into?

But surroundings were appearance related, she argued. They didn't necessarily say anything about the person himself.

So, just how well did she know the person himself?

She didn't know much about his private life, his friends, his work.

But she did know a little about his background from what Howard had said over the years. She knew he'd been understandably devastated by the death of his parents. She knew he'd acted out his grief by trying to appear tough as nails, that he'd spent a year fighting with every boy who looked cross-eyed at him, but that after that year he'd come out of it to be a kid Howard had been as proud of as any of his own three.

She knew that as an adult Bucky Horvat had been good to Howard and Aggie. He was conscientious about birthdays and anniversaries. He was family oriented and always the first person to step in and help—she recalled the time when Howard's youngest daughter had gotten divorced and gone through a rough time getting on her feet, emotionally and financially. Bucky had been the one to supplement her income and call her with as much regularity as Aggie and Howard had.

But what did she know firsthand? Blythe asked herself.

She knew he was kind and compassionate. So kind and compassionate that even believing she'd maliciously taken Howard's formula hadn't kept him from comforting her when she'd been upset over the things that were happening with his uncle.

She knew he was loyal and cared deeply enough to go to great lengths to help those closest to him. Not many people would drop everything in their own life to play bodyguard, so they could retrieve something that belonged to someone else.

And as she thought about it, she knew he really wasn't the kind of man to have cold-bloodedly seduced her just to gain access to the formula or to make love to her for any reason other than desire for her. Bruised pride, she guessed, had put that shadow over what had happened between them.

Most of all she knew he was a man she felt comfortable with. A man she enjoyed. A man she found to be warm and interesting and funny and pleasant. A man she loved and wanted so much that the wanting was almost alive inside her.

She leaned slightly forward and breathed in the scent of after-shave coming from the leather bag.

Maybe she knew more about him than she realized. At least more of the things that mattered. And the rest, well, maybe it was okay to learn slowly about the details of his work, his friends, or whatever she didn't yet know about his past.

Blythe couldn't resist running just her fingertips over the leather of his shaving bag.

Maybe what she didn't know about him wasn't as important as what she did.

"A couple of hours' sleep in my own bed and I've gone crazy," she whispered.

Maybe she'd grown sane.

One of Lee's messages on her answering machine played over again in her mind. Fooling her about who he was and why he was in her life wasn't something Lee had done to hurt her or to make a fool out of her. It was something he'd done to help his uncle. Just the way what she'd done had been to help Howard.

Lee had forgiven her for the pain and problems her taking EASY had caused because of her reasons for it. Couldn't she forgive him the same way?

After all, pride made a poor bedfellow. Especially when it replaced the man she loved.

She did love Lee. She could deny it to herself until the end of time, but that wouldn't change things. Hadn't she successfully denied it for the past three weeks? Hadn't she chased away thoughts of him with chemical equations and notations and concentrating on Howard's formula? And what difference had that made? One look at him had made her collapse into sobs.

"Admit it," she challenged the Dopp Kit.

Okay. She loved Lee Farrell. Horvat. Bucky. The bridge builder. She loved him more than she had ever loved Jerry Nickles. More than she had ever loved anyone.

And how, that internal voice of sanity asked her, could she leave him alone to face one of the most difficult things in his life—the deterioration of the man who'd raised him?

She couldn't. She belonged at Lee's side, doing whatever she could for him and for Howard. But it was more than the fact that they belonged together. That was where she wanted to be.

"Think he'd have Blythe for breakfast?" she asked the shaving bag.

Had he meant all the things he'd said on the answering machine? Or had he given up on her?

She was afraid even to think that.

She grabbed two towels and a washcloth and closed the linen closet door as if that leather bag might tell her it was too late.

It couldn't be too late. It just couldn't. Hadn't he taken that step toward her today? Hadn't he called her name?

She had to hope he hadn't just been about to shake her hand and thank her for her work on EASY.

She turned on the shower and stepped into the bath tub. The warm spray of the water felt good and brought with it memories of another shower. With Lee. In what she now knew was the bathroom off his bedroom.

She'd been fooled, all right—by herself—to ever believe she could live without what that man did to her. Physically, mentally and emotionally.

It seemed as if every nerve was on the surface of her skin as she lathered her body, then closed her eyes and let the water rain over her to rinse off.

Maybe she should go out to Genesee tonight....

No, not a good idea, she decided and stepped out of the spray to wash her hair. She wasn't sure she could find his house in the dark. And she didn't want to seem too desperate, just in case...

It was going to be a long wait for morning.

With her hair rinsed she turned off the water and the sound of her doorbell came into the sudden silence. She froze and whispered, "Howard."

What if Lee hadn't had a chance to tell his uncle that she'd given EASY back yet? Or what if he had told his old mentor, but Howard hadn't retained the informa tion? What if he'd forgotten all that had gone on since she'd taken the formula and was here in the same frame of mind he'd been in the night he'd broken her window and the night he'd shouted from her front lawn? At least the first night she hadn't been home, and on the second occasion she'd had Lee here to deal with him.

A second ring sounded and a chill reminded her she was dripping wet. She reached beyond the shower cur tain for her towels, wondering what she should do as she wrapped one around her head and used the other to dry off.

She could lock the bathroom door, stay there and hope that even if he got into the house, he wouldn't get into the bathroom.

But if he did get into the bathroom, she wouldn't have any escape route at all.

"Ridiculous," she said, stepping onto the bath mat as the doorbell sounded for the third time. This was Howard, for crying out loud, not some serial killer. And now that EASY wasn't here anymore, what was at risk? she asked herself as she put on her red terry cloth robe and tied it at her waist.

Until now it had been important for Howard not to get hold of the formula. But did she really think he might do her some harm? Maybe she was being naive, but she didn't. Howard might be angry, confused, might not remember that she didn't have EASY anymore, might even break a few things if worse came to worst, but when she really thought about it, she just didn't believe she was in any personal danger from him. And if everything worked out the way she hoped it would with Lee, she'd be facing Howard sooner or later, anyway.

The doorbell rang three more times in rapid succession.

Blythe took a deep breath and went into the living room, turning lights on as she passed the switches. It didn't help the racing of her pulse to hear what sounded like a heavy fist beating on her door, just as she reached for the knob, but she opened it, anyway. "Howard..."

It wasn't Howard.

It was Lee.

Her heartbeat, instead of slowing down, raced ever faster.

He had on jeans and a shirt that he hadn't bothered to button or tuck in, and his hair looked the way it had in the mornings when he first got up. It seemed clear he'd made a fast track from his bed to her porch, and the frown on his beard-shadowed face suggested that he wasn't too happy.

"Did something happen?" Blythe asked, her mentor still not far from her thoughts.

"Yes, dammit," Lee said, yanking the screen door open to storm into the house and slam the wooden door closed behind him. He jammed his hand through his hair and shouted, "Look, I'm not all that complicated a guy. What you saw during the time we spent together is basically what and who I am—"

"I know," she said, cutting him off in full flight.

"You know?"

Blythe couldn't help taking a glance down at the strip of golden hair showing between the open ends of his shirt and following it all the way to the button on the waistband of his jeans. "Did you just get out of bed to say that?" she asked.

"I couldn't sleep. I kept tossing and turning and thinking that I couldn't let something that isn't even the damn truth keep us from having what I know was meant to be."

Blythe shrugged. "Okay."

"Okay?" he repeated, still shouting in spite of her quiet response.

"That's what I said. Okay."

He shifted his weight onto one hip, frowned more fiercely and asked in a more normal voice, "Okay meaning you agree?"

She nodded. "As a matter of fact, at the crack of dawn I was going to be on your doorstep, telling you almost the same thing. I realized that I know more about you than I thought I did. It occurred to me that even without facts and figures I know what kind of a man you are and that's more important. It's just that for awhile I felt as if you'd used my weakness just to get your hands on EASY."

He smiled. "Do you have a weakness for me?"

"I'm afraid so."

"And you actually thought I—"

"Had seduced me just so I'd drop my guard," she added, finishing for him. "It was quite a blow to find out that the person I'd just slept with wasn't who I thought he was."

"Conceded." His expression relaxed slightly. "But you're all mixed-up if you think the personal stuff had anything to do with the formula. It's exactly the opposite. I was fighting madly against what I felt for you, because it was making it harder and harder to think you were a research pirate. I was going out of my mind, worrying how I could be falling in love with that kind of person."

"But you really were falling in love?"

"Absolutely." He angled his head to look directly into her eyes. "Am I forgiven for playing Halloween in May?"

"Yes."

"And you love me?"

"I love you," she confirmed.

"So you'll marry me?"

"So I'll marry you."

He smiled then, a slow, lazy smile as he reached one hand to the towel wrapped around her head and pulled it off, sending her damp hair tumbling around her shoulders. "I'll marry you, too," he informed her.

"Gee, thanks!" She laughed.

He hooked his fingers in the belt of her robe and pulled her to him, loosely draping his arms around her hips and locking his hands at the base of her spine. "How did you happen to come to this revelation? You certainly didn't seem to want anything to do with me as late as this afternoon."

"Some things just clicked into place," she said vaguely. How could she tell him the catalyst had been his Dopp Kit?

"And those things didn't click into place until today? What about all the messages I've been leaving on your machine for the past three weeks? Didn't they do anything to move you?"

"I didn't hear them until after I delivered EASY to you this afternoon. I've been hiding out at Gib's sister-in-law's apartment."

He dropped his head to the top of hers. "And all this time I thought you were here, ignoring my calls and not answering your door because you didn't want anything to do with me."

He pulled her in close and just held her for awhile. Blythe listened to his heartbeat and let the warmth of his body seep into her.

When he spoke again his voice was low, gentle. "It's hard to believe something this good could come out of something so bad."

"I know," she said, sliding her hands up inside his shirt to his broad back. "Another part of what I realized tonight was that I wanted to be with you every step of the way through Howard's illness."

He pressed his lips to her crown. "Good, because that's where I want you."

"I'm sorry I was right."

"So am I. But if you hadn't done what you did, who knows how long my aunt would have gone on denying there was anything wrong?"

"Then she did notice that there was a problem?"

"Yes. Didn't I tell you that?"

"You didn't tell me much of anything."

"I was too busy trying to keep myself from tying you to a chair to get you to stay with me."

"You didn't tell me you were kinky."

"Only if the need arises."

She smiled and kissed his chest. "Anything arising now?"

"Already arisen."

"Sounds like a rock band."

"I can rock." And he did, mostly with his hips into hers. "It's been a long three weeks," he said in a suddenly husky voice.

"Mmm," she agreed. Or maybe she was just commenting on how wonderful it felt for him to slip his hands inside her robe and lay his palms against her bare back.

"I love you, Blythe."

"I love you, too, Lee Farrell Bucky Horvat."

"Keep it simple, call me darling."

"I thought I'd call you husband."

"That works, too."

So would everything else from now on, Blythe reflected, as he led her off to her bedroom.

* * * * *

FOUR UNIQUE SERIES
FOR EVERY WOMAN YOU ARE...

Silhouette Romance®

Love, at its most tender, provocative, emotional... in stories that will make you laugh and cry while bringing you the magic of falling in love.

6 titles per month

Silhouette Special Edition®

Sophisticated, substantial and packed with emotion, these powerful novels of life and love will capture your imagination and steal your heart.

6 titles per month

SILHOUETTE *Desire*®

Open the door to romance and passion. Humorous, emotional, compelling—yet always a believable and sensuous story—Silhouette Desire never fails to deliver on the promise of love.

6 titles per month

SILHOUETTE·INTIMATE·MOMENTS®

Enter a world of excitement, of romance heightened by suspense, adventure and the passions every woman dreams of. Let us sweep you away.

4 titles per month